The

P

Collect all of The Pony Whisperer books:

The Pony Whisperer

PRIZE PROBLEMS

JANET RISING

sourcebooks
jabberwocky

Published by Sourcebooks Jabberwocky, an imprint of Sourcebooks, Inc.
(630) 961-3900
Fax: (630) 961-2168
www.jabberwockykids.com

First published in Great Britain in 2010 by Hodder Children's Books.

Library of Congress Cataloging-in-Publication data is on file with the publisher.

Source of Production: Versa Press, East Peoria, Illinois, USA
Date of Production: November 2011
Run Number: 16250

Printed and bound in the United States of America.
VP 10 9 8 7 6 5 4 3 2 1

For Eleanor, Margaret, and David

CHAPTER 1

"YOU WILL NEVER, IN a million years, guess what this is!" shouted Bean, bursting through the tack room door and waving an envelope in our direction.

Dee-Dee, who was searching through her tack box in disgust to see how many yellow ribbons her mother had thrown in there, didn't want to know. "Close the door, it's freezing out there!" she shrieked.

"A letter," declared Katy, shoving a chip in her mouth and crunching, barely glancing up from her book about cross-country jumping. She sat on a pile of pony rugs, her feet propped up on an empty bucket, tendrils of red hair escaping her hat.

"Well, yes, technically," confirmed Bean, irritated, slamming the door behind her. "But what's *in* the letter?" she teased, holding the envelope by the corner and wafting it in Katy's direction.

"Words?" I suggested, dipping my hand into the chip bag and pulling out the biggest one, which immediately snapped in two. Of course, the big piece floated to the ground and I watched dismayed as Squish, the yard's greyhound, pounced and gulped it down in one.

"Oh no," said Dee, holding up her fingers so she

wouldn't lose count, "dogs aren't supposed to have salt. Squish will die a horrible death."

"What, from half a chip? Unlikely," I said. "Besides, it was nacho cheese, not ready salted."

"It's still loaded with salt," said Dee accusingly. "Oh no, here's a white one! When did I get that?" she wailed, aiming the unwanted ribbon at the empty feed sack we use as a trash can, and missing.

"Jeez, most people would be thrilled to come fourth in the classes you go to. Gimme another chip," I said, stretching over.

Katy shook her head and snatched the bag away. "Don't think so, you've just wasted that one!"

"Hey, what about my letter!" exclaimed Bean.

"How are we supposed to know what's in it?" whined Dee. "It's your letter."

"Oh, you all think you're so smart—only you're not," smirked Bean. "I am," she added, flicking back her blond hair and sticking her nose in the air.

That did get our attention. Bean isn't famous for being smart. She's in a world of her own most of the time with a unique way of being with us in body, but not in spirit, if you know what I mean.

"How come?" I asked, intrigued.

Bean pointed to her chest and lifted her chin. "You're looking at Charlotte Beanie, winner of a riding vacation—in that competition I entered in *Pony* mag. Don't tell me you've forgotten!"

I hadn't. It was forever ago, last autumn, and the reason I hadn't forgotten was because Bean had pestered us with most of the questions. The way I remembered it, I had answered most of them.

"No way!" said Dee, her mouth dropping open.

"But no one ever wins those things!" cried Katy, letting the chip bag fall. Squish took advantage of the situation and wolfed down the rest of the contents, salt and all. Dee was too flabbergasted to notice.

"That's exactly what you said then—but I did, so there!" Bean replied with justifiable smugness.

"Let's see!" I said, grabbing the envelope and pulling out the letter. "Bean's right," I said, scanning the words. "Congratulations! Blah, blah, a vacation at High Grove Farm, blah, blah five days blah, blah, for you and a friend, blah, blah the vacation must be taken during the Spring Break," I read out, "and is nontransferable—what does that mean?"

"It means you can't give it to anyone else," said Katy, looking over my shoulder.

"Like I was going to!" Bean snorted.

"You seem very calm," I remarked. "If I won a riding vacation, I'd be bouncing off the walls."

"I was earlier, when the letter arrived, but I've gotten used to the idea now," Bean said, folding the letter carefully and returning it to the envelope. "What you see here is me, playing it cool."

"Who are you taking with you—one of your sisters?" Dee asked.

Bean made a sound like a deflating balloon. "Yeah, right!" she exclaimed. "Actually, seeing as how you helped me with so many of the questions, Pia, I wondered whether you'd like to come. After all, I wouldn't have won without your help. I hope you don't mind," she looked at Katy and Dee, "but I can only take one person with me and it seems right as Pia helped me so much."

I felt my lower jaw dropping in surprise. I so totally hadn't seen that coming!

Dee huffed loudly. "I'd love to be able to ride an ordinary pony for a week, away from my mom, doing fun stuff instead of endless show schooling on Dolly," she said.

"Don't start all that ordinary pony talk again!" snapped Katy. "It's so…so insulting to all our ponies!"

"Oh, you know what I mean," wailed Dee.

I held my breath. Was Bean's win going to cause friction between us? But then Dee shrugged her shoulders. "Oh well, as Pia helped you," she sighed, "then I suppose it's only fair."

"Yeah, anyway, I don't want to ride any other pony but Bluey," added Katy. She sounded a bit sniffy about it, but I knew Katy was telling the truth. She adored her chunky blue roan gelding, especially as he'd restored her confidence by proving to be amazing at cross-country jumping. Bluey loved jumping more than anything—except Katy. Dee, on the other hand, had a whole new show season to look forward to on her gorgeous dappled gray mare, Dolly Daydream. After qualifying for the Horse of the Year Show last year, Dee—or rather Dee's mom, Sophie—was determined to do so again. And do better than the incredible ninth place they'd achieved at Nationals. Just getting to HOYS was, as Sophie never tired of saying (usually overheard on her cell phone to one of her showing friends), a significant achievement in itself. If they didn't qualify again this year, Sophie had already decided it would be nothing less than an almighty injustice. The only problem was that Dee was never allowed to do anything else with Dolly. Her mom just wouldn't let her risk it in case Dolly injured herself or got a splint, and so Dee missed out on all the fun things we all did with our so-called ordinary ponies. I know I wouldn't have swapped my ordinary pony, Drummer, for all of Dee's ribbons—whatever color they happened to be!

"Well?" Bean said to me, her eyebrows disappearing into her blond bangs. "Why aren't you bouncing off the walls? I assume you'd like to come with me?"

"*Would I?*" I almost screamed, trying not to sound too excited as Katy and Dee were being left out. "Yes, yes, I *would*. Do you mean it?"

"Yeah, of course. I'll let the people at the mag know. We'll have an awesome time!"

"Oh, you are lucky!" said Dee, half whining—but only half. "You'll have so much fun and I bet you get gorgeous ponies and have midnight feasts and everything. Everyone I've ever known who's gone on a riding vacation has said it's just the best thing ever. My friend Cindy went on one

5

and said they had virtually no one in charge and just ran wild for a week. She didn't even take a bath!"

"And that's your idea of a great time?" asked Katy, who still sounded a bit put out and was looking at Dee with a pained expression. "Going native?"

"Oh, lighten up," snapped Dee. "Cindy said they rode the ponies to the beach and they had a gymkhana at the end of the week, and she totally fell in love with her pony and cried buckets when she had to leave at the end, and everything. She couldn't wait to go back the following year with all her new friends."

"Can we take Drummer and Tiffany?" I asked, thinking how cool it would be for Drum to have a vacation, too. I didn't particularly want to fall in love with any other pony but my wonderful bay gelding.

Bean shook her head and made a sad face. "Nah—I've already asked. No go. We'll be riding the center's ponies."

"Will someone look after Drummer for me?" I asked, aware that it was asking a lot—I was going with Bean, and Dee and Katy weren't, and now I expected them to look after Drum. Plus I felt slightly guilty at how readily I was willing to dump him for a riding vacation. But honestly, how often does an opportunity like this crop up? I know, I know, like NEVER!

"Oh, and Tiffany," added Bean. "I totally forgot about that. Will someone be nice enough to look after my baby, too?"

Katy put her lips together like she was sucking a lemon

and slowly shook her head at us like teachers at school do when they spot you're wearing nail polish or your shoes have a heel just a tad higher than regulations allow. "Don't you worry," she said huffily, "we'll do it. You just go off and have a great time, never mind about us, or the ponies or anything. Just so long as you two enjoy yourselves!"

Bean and I just looked at her, aghast.

Katy rolled her eyes when she saw our faces. "I'm kidding!" she laughed. "Go and have a great time. I've got two hunter trials booked for Bluey and me at Easter so I can't go anywhere. Besides, I'll enjoy looking after Drummer, he's cute!"

"You wouldn't say that if you could hear what he says!" I replied, relieved Katy was being so cool about looking after Drum.

How do I know what Drummer says? It's all because of Epona, a tiny stone statue of a Celtic goddess of horses which—don't ask me how—allows me to hear what horses and ponies are saying. I found Epona—or maybe Epona found me—when I first moved to Laurel Farm, the stable where I keep Drum. Only one other person knows that my ability to hear horse-speak is due to the 2,000 year-old artifact—everyone else believes I possess special powers and they call me the Pony Whisperer, which means I'm always translating their ponies' thoughts and conversations for them. At first, I thought it would be a lot of fun and my way to fame, fortune, and celebrity status, but after a few dicey situations I no longer volunteer my so-called pony-whispering powers to strangers if I can possibly help it. It just causes trouble.

"I'd better get my mom to talk to your parents," I said to Bean. "You know what parents are like, always wanting to know the ins and outs of everything."

"Oooeeeooo!" Dee butted in. "Get your people to talk to my people! You sound like some big Hollywood mogul!"

"Hollywood what?" asked Bean.

"What's your land line number?" I asked, pulling out my cell to add it to my address book.

"Er, I think I can remember it," said Bean, screwing up her face in concentration. "I guess you're right, they'll want to have a chat about it. Get your mom to call them tonight. Oh no, wait a minute."

"What?" My thumb hovered over the number pad.

"I think they've got something tonight."

"Thing?"

"Yeah, definitely a thing."

We expected more. As usual, we didn't get it.

"What?" Bean said as we all stared at her.

"What sort of thing?" Katy asked exasperated.

"Oh, um…that's it! Haley has a concert. But hold on, I think they're not going until about seven, so get her to call before that. Mom knows I'm going to ask you and they're fine with it. They'll love me being away for a week during Spring Break so they can all get on with their artsy stuff together without me cluttering up the place."

Bean's family is mega artistic. Her father is a musician,

her mother a sculptor, one of her sisters plays the violin, and the other loves to paint. I don't just mean dabbling in these things, I mean they are all totally serious about them. Gifted. Bean's talents and interests lie in the direction of riding. None of her family is the slightest bit interested in horses and Bean's palomino pony Tiffany provides a great excuse for Bean to escape from activities she just doesn't get. She says the rest of her family is glad to see the back of her when she goes (escapes, she calls it) to the stable.

I pedaled my bike home to brief Mom and get her to call and arrange things. I so wanted to go on the riding vacation with Bean! I mean, one minute I was looking forward to spring giving winter the push, and wishing that Drummer's summer coat would hurry up and grow through his clip, and hoping he would stop bucking because he was feeling the cold, and the next minute I had a riding vacation to look forward to in a matter of weeks. It was so excellent. I'd always wanted to go on a riding vacation. I could hardly believe it!

CHAPTER 2

I WAS SO EXCITED, I pedaled my bike far too fast, cornered our gateway like a Hollywood stunt rider and, bouncing the front wheel off the step, just missed head-butting our front door and ending up wearing our mailbox for a hat.

"Wow bike, impressive!" I told it as I wobbled out of the saddle. "You can buck almost as well as Drummer!"

My mom, annoyingly oblivious to my obvious excitement and bubbling important news, had her cell phone jammed to her ear. And she was clearly in no hurry to wind up the conversation. Which could only mean one thing: she was talking with one of her gentleman friends.

My mom collects boyfriends like Drummer collects straw in his tail. She has three at the moment. Oh no, wait a minute, I forgot, she only has two now, ever since I answered the door to the geeky dark-haired, bespectacled one with the question, "Which one are you, David, Simon or Leonard?" He got huffy and the date was off. What's more, he took his chocolates with him, which was the real bummer. It was David, in case you were wondering (as if!). Simon and Leonard are still in the running. Well, more hovering around, actually. I don't think Mom's that smitten with either of them.

It's since Mom got her new Facebook page. Carol (her influential-and-not-in-a-good-way friend) took a smoldering photo of her to post up and the offers have come flooding in. Soooo embarrassing. I mean, when she was a member of her internet dating club at least no one else could log on and watch her list of weirdo friends getting ever longer. Now her love life is anyone's business. I just answer the door and let them in. No names, no questions, no nothing.

It's called denial, apparently, and I'm in it.

Thing is, my mom and dad are divorced and while Dad is having a great time with his new girlfriend Lyn (aka Skinny Lynny—there's more fat on a chip), Mom is still looking for Mr. Right. I mean, Mr. Right 2.0, seeing as the first Mr. Right (my dad) ran off with a much younger woman (Lyn—are you getting all this?) from work. I don't know why she needs a Mr. R., but she seems to think she does. Hence the Facebook thing. Hence the suitors. Hence the mix-ups when she decides that limiting her male friends to one at a time is so yesterday.

Anyway, Mom eventually got off the phone (after much face-pulling and gesticulating by me), flicked her newly highlighted blond hair back, narrowed her eyes, stuck her hands on her hips and demanded to know why I was buzzing round her like a demented fly.

So I told her.

Now, I thought that she'd whoop a bit and we'd dance about our tiny house with glee at the huge news that I had a riding vacation in the bag—and she didn't have to pay

for it—which was the clincher, as far as I was concerned
'cause how many times is expense trotted out as an excuse
not to do something? And I know we don't have the spare
cash for such things.

Only she didn't. She sucked her cheeks in a bit and
kept asking totally pointless questions. You know the sort
of thing—where was it? Who was in charge? What quali-
fications did they have? How did we know they weren't
weirdos, and why didn't Charlotte want to take one of
her sisters? Some I could answer, and some I couldn't,
so I gave her Bean's phone number and asked her to call
her parents. Honestly, what a fuss! You'd have thought
Bean had offered me a human sacrifice weekend with
Vampires Anonymous!

I must have crossed my fingers, toes, legs, arms—
practically everything—while she spoke to Bean's mom (I
almost tied myself in a knot) but eventually, she hung up
and said she didn't see why, in principle, I couldn't go.

Phew! I immediately rang Bean on my cell.

"We're so going!" she yelled. Then I had a thought.

"Why not get your parents to drop you off here on their
way to the concert thing—we can give High Grove Farm's
website a good going-over."

"Good idea. MOOOOM!"

I winced and held my cell at arm's length, my ear ringing.

"I'll be by just after seven!" Bean said (at least I think
that's what she said, my hearing having been severely com-
promised) and hung up.

When she arrived, we sat at the computer and munched chocolate chip cookies. We just bought groceries, so supplies were up! I was hoping we'd be able to make a hole in the cherry Danishes I'd spotted in the cupboard, too. Thank goodness my mom had ditched her keep-fit and health kick regime when she stopped going out with her gym instructor. Now what was needed was for Simon or Leonard to be like a pastry chef or something—that would be awesome! That was just one of the many problems with Mom dating—she tended to morph into whatever her latest boyfriend was into. I just prayed she wouldn't fall in love with a math teacher or a child psychologist. Imagine!

"Here it is, High Grove Farm," Bean announced as the sunshine-yellow-colored website flashed up before our eyes. "Our mission statement: Happy holidays for horses and humans!"

"Quick, click on ponies," Bean said, pointing to the menu and spitting chocolate chip crumbs into the keyboard.

I clicked and a picture of a chestnut pony with a white star appeared. We leaned forward in our seats, full of anticipation.

"Sorrel is our impeccably bred chestnut mare," I read out. "Formerly a top show pony, perfectly schooled Sorrel now teaches our guests the finer points of horsemanship."

"What a gorgeous thoroughbred head," said Bean. "I wouldn't mind learning the finer points of horsemanship, whatever that means. Who's next?"

I scrolled down. A piebald head looked out of the screen.

At least, he tried to; a curtain of white forelock made it tricky. The caption read:

BOLD AND BRASH, HARRY USED TO BE A WORK-ING PONY IN THE CITY PULLING A CART FOR A STREET VENDOR. A REAL CHARACTER, HE TRIES HIS HARDEST AT ANYTHING AND EVERYTHING!

"My great-gran used to run out to feed the horses in the old days when they came around," said Bean.

"Harry must be ancient!"

"Says here he's twelve, so that doesn't stack up," replied Bean.

"He looks fun, I wouldn't mind riding him," I said, scrolling down to the next pony, which was a gray—almost white.

SHADOW IS OUR LONGEST-SERVING RESIDENT, AND IS A GREAT FAVORITE WITH OUR MORE NERVOUS RIDERS. DEAR AND PATIENT SHADOW NEVER PUTS A HOOF WRONG!

"Ahhh, he's cute, but I hope I don't get him," mused Bean, reaching for another cookie. "I want something with a bit of life! Who's next?"

Bean's pony Tiffany had plenty of life in her. The trouble was, it mostly took the form of spooking at perfectly ordinary things like trees, or snorting at a leaf that was just ever-so-slightly wonky.

"This one's called Dot-2-Dot," I read as an Appaloosa head appeared. Her spots were arranged willy-nilly all over her face, and we could see the whites of her eyes, in true Appaloosa fashion.

DOT-2-DOT IS THE NEW GIRL ON THE BLOCK. ALTHOUGH YOUNG, DOTTY IS LEARNING FAST AND LOVES TO PLEASE.

"I hope I don't get Dot either," said Bean, screwing up her nose.

"Why not? She looks gorgeous, I love Appaloosas— don't tell Drummer, though!"

"I want a dirt-colored one. It would give me a rest from grooming a light pony, like Tiff," explained Bean. I neglected to point out how she didn't actually groom Tiff much. Instead I said, "Dot-2-Dot is a cool name! Who's next?"

A gray pony with a dark gray mane and a pink snip—a tiny marking between his nostrils—peered out at us from the screen.

LIVELY SPROUT LOVES JUMPING AND HAS PLENTY OF TRICKS UP HIS SLEEVE. LIFE'S NEVER BORING WITH SPROUT AROUND!

"Up his sleeve?" said Bean. "It sounds like he wears a sweater. Can you get sweaters for ponies?"

"What kind of name is Sprout for a pony?" I said.

"Perhaps he's from Brussels," suggested Bean, and we both giggled.

"I hope you don't get him," I said. "Together, you'd make a bean sprout! Get it?"

"That's so not funny," mumbled Bean.

I thought it was. "They all sound like profiles of my mom's potential boyfriends on her internet dating site," I said, changing the subject.

"Whatever are you two doing?" asked my clairvoyant mom. She must be clairvoyant because she had a plate of cherry Danishes with her.

"It's the High Grove Farm ponies," I told her. "Don't they look adorable?"

"Which ones are yours, do you know?" Mom asked, peering at the screen.

"No, not yet," sighed Bean. "But they all look great!"

"There's one more," I said as a bay head came into view. It looked a little like Drummer. I did hope Drum wouldn't mind me deserting him. I hadn't told him yet.

MEET CHEROKEE, OUR STUNNING TRICOLORED PONY. BAY WITH WHITE SPLASHES, CHEROKEE CAME TO US FROM A HORSE RESCUE ORGANIZATION. HE'S NOW FULLY SETTLED IN AND LOVES HIS NEW JOB!

"Oh, I do so want Cherokee!" I wailed.

"I wonder what happened for him to wind up in need of rescuing," Bean said.

Mom helped herself to a Danish. "I'm sure they're all wonderful," she said, giving me a look, "although not quite as wonderful as Drummer."

I grinned at her. I love the way Mom's loyal to Drum.

"Any chance of clicking on accommodation?" asked Mom, looking intently at the screen. I clicked, hoping it wouldn't show anything that made Mom change her mind about me going. I don't know what I thought it might be—tents or a camper van or an old, falling down barn. I just expected the worst.

"Mmmm," said Mom, reading the blurb. "Farmhouse accommodation in a dormitory. All our guests live as family with good, wholesome home cooking. Please advise of any dietary requirements or allergies. Sample menu—click on that link, would you Pia?"

I obliged. I was quite anxious to see a sample menu, too.

It wasn't exactly *Top Chef* but there seemed plenty of it. Fish sticks, burgers, lasagna, pot pies, chicken, salads, dessert. Plus a snack shop selling cookies and sweets. Barbecues held every week, it said.

"It doesn't look like we'll starve," said Bean.

Satisfied with the website descriptions, plus the pictures of the farmhouse and images of happy guests digging into High Grove Farm fare, Mom decided she had something else to do and left. We went back to the ponies menu to take another look.

"I've got a fabulous new polo shirt and some gorgeous leather riding gloves I'm saving to take to High Grove Farm," Bean told me. "Oh, and how cool will it be, you being able to tell everyone what the ponies are saying!" she added.

My heart sank. "I'd rather not," I said. "It might make things difficult."

"Oh, Pia!" wailed Bean. "You'll tell me what my pony says, won't you?"

I nodded furiously. "Of course. But I'd rather keep the pony-whispering thing a secret, if you don't mind. Things always seem to go wrong whenever people know about it."

Bean sighed. "OK, if that's the way you want it," she

agreed. "I can't make up my mind which pony I like best. Harry looks so cheeky, and Sprout looks like he'd be really cool—but then Sorrel looks super classy—and she's the right color, too. I'm so looking forward to a vacation from grooming!"

I felt excitement rising in my chest. I would need to make sure to pack Epona so I could talk to whichever pony I got for the week. "I don't mind who I ride," I said, grinning. "This riding vacation is going to be the totally, totally coolest thing ever!"

Chapter 3

"Welcome to High Grove Farm!" boomed a tubby woman bearing down upon us and wiping her hands on her apron. She wore her graying blond hair in two braids, which made her look like an aging Viking woman, and her rosy cheeks were shiny like apples. "I'm Mrs. Reeve—you must be Amber and Zoe."

"No, we're not," said Bean bluntly. "We're Bean and Pia."

"This is Charlotte and her friend Pia," Bean's mom corrected her, giving her a look. Bean gazed skyward in despair.

Bean's mom and dad had driven us to High Grove Farm. It had taken three hours and all the time we'd sat in the back of the car and talked ponies. Bean's parents had talked about her mom's latest commission from some rich guy who had seen her work in a gallery. He'd been quite specific, apparently, about where he wanted to put the sculpture—it had to be a certain size. This didn't sit too well with Bean's mom.

"They don't understand how an artist needs to be inspired," she had complained, wafting her hand about in what looked to me like a particularly artistic way. Either that or she had a smell under her nose. "I can't just produce something to order like that. There's no knowing exactly how it will turn out, it's all fluid and organic. I have to feel the piece and let the process guide me. I don't control it, it controls me."

I didn't understand what her mom was talking about, not being artistic myself. I'd seen some of her works and they missed my brain by about three miles. She took everyday objects and sort of did things with them. When I'd visited Bean's house, I'd thought a beaten-up bicycle in the garden with twigs and bits of rubber stuck all over it had been something the family had thrown out, rather than a particularly raved-over piece her mother had created, which had been accepted for a prestigious exhibition somewhere. Wouldn't you think anyone with talent would sculpt something fabulous, like horses? I mean, who could get tired of making horses? But no, Bean's mom has a very modern approach to sculpture, which I just don't get.

Bean's father had a gripe of his own—about some concert he had lined up. He'd complained about how people expected artists to just perform without the necessary practice.

"It's exactly the same thing," Bean's mom had declared, her arms wafting in earnest. "People who are not artistic have no concept of how we work, Bernard. It's not something you can turn on like a tap. They don't understand how an artist needs to be inspired."

"So true, Ingrid," Bean's father had agreed, nodding furiously and braking hard at a set of traffic lights so that our seat belts cut us practically in two. "They expect a five-star performance with only a two-star practice."

"And then they're disappointed!" Bean's mom had concluded, her hand falling on to her lap.

I had so felt for Bean if this was the sort of conversation she was subjected to all the time. No wonder she'd been looking forward to the riding vacation. As the traffic lights had turned green and Bernard angrily crunched the gears and accelerated, throwing us back into the seats, my thoughts had flown back to Drummer and our parting that morning. I'd sniffed a bit and welled up, blinking back the tears. I hated leaving Drummer behind and wished he could have been included in our adventure.

"Katy will see to your every need," I'd told him, stroking his thick, black mane.

"Don't miss your ride," he'd replied, between mouthfuls of hay.

"I wouldn't go and leave you like this," I'd gulped, "only I've always, always wanted to go on a riding vacation. It's going to be an ambition fulfilled," I'd added, dramatically.

"Yeah, well, you always wanted to be a horsey celebrity," Drummer had reminded me, "and we all know how well that turned out!"

Suddenly, leaving my pony behind had seemed a lot easier. "Don't be too upset!" I'd remarked.

"I'll do my best. You'd better go while I can still hold it together," Drum had returned his full attention to his feed bag. "Shut the door on your way out."

Mrs. Reeve beamed at us. Her mouth seemed to take up almost half of her face. "Charlotte and Pia. Of course—Charlotte is our competition winner, aren't you? Clever girl! Well, we'll make sure you have a wonderful time here at High Grove Farm. All my guests have a wonderful time!"

Mr. and Mrs. Beanie each shook Mrs. Reeve's hand and Mrs. Beanie asked whether they might be able to see where Charlotte and I would be sleeping.

"Of course, follow me and bring your luggage. Two of the others are already here and they're dying to meet you both," gushed Mrs. Reeve, walking back into the old farmhouse and beckoning us to follow her.

We went in through the kitchen. "This is where we all take our meals," boomed Mrs. Reeve, waving toward a huge pine table with wooden benches either side, before we followed her up two sets of wide stairs to a huge room in the roof which housed six beds, three on either side of the room.

"And there are two shower rooms, through there," waved Mrs. Reeve, smiling at Bean and me, "and there—so no excuses about lines!" She nodded knowingly to Bean's parents, assuming Bean and I couldn't wait to give the soap a miss for five days—the nerve! There were two suitcases next to beds on opposite sides, already claimed, so we dumped our cases on two adjacent beds under the eaves nearest to the window and peered out. Below us we could see a farmyard with stable doors opening on to it and beyond, a schooling paddock. Open countryside surrounded us. It was gorgeous!

"Can't see any ponies," muttered Bean, scanning the view.

Bean's parents declared themselves satisfied with the arrangements and we all trooped down the stairs. Mrs. Reeve puffed a bit and flicked back a braid.

"You girls run along to the stable yard and make friends with Grace and Ellie—and Annabelle's there too. They're all dying to meet you!"

"Good-bye, Charlotte," said Mrs. Beanie, leaning down to kiss Bean on the cheek.

"Have a good time—and you Pia," her father said gruffly, glancing at his watch.

"Thank you Mr. Beanie," I said. "And thank you very much for letting me come on this vacation with Be—Charlotte."

Bean's mother smiled. "You're very welcome, Pia. I hope you both have a lovely time. Don't forget to clean your teeth thoroughly every night, Charlotte, will you?"

We fled to the stable yard. Stables filled two sides of it; the third had doors marked tack room, feed room and chill-out room; the fence and gate filled the last.

As the gate clicked shut a tall young woman wearing a lemon-colored polo shirt, checked jodhpurs and long boots appeared from the chill-out room. Her auburn hair was tied back and she wore quite a lot of eye make-up. She looked too clean to be on a stable yard. She looked a bit like she ought to have been on the TV instead, talking about the weather. Or, as my dad always complains, lying about the weather.

"Hello girls!" she called, smiling earnestly. "I'm Annabelle, so if you want to know anything, just ask me. You must be Zoe and Amber!"

"No, we're still not them," said Bean a bit testily. "I'm Bean and this is Pia."

Annabelle's smile froze and she tilted her head on one side and blinked rapidly in confusion. Clearly, she didn't take too well to being wrong. "Bean?" she said, frowning, "I thought Charlotte was coming with Pia."

"I'm Charlotte, but everyone calls me Bean."

"Your parents don't," I hissed.

"They don't count," Bean hissed back.

"Well, come and meet Ellie and Grace," said Annabelle, waving us over, her smile resurrected. "They're dying to meet you!"

A girl with very long brown hair appeared at the door. She wore jodhpurs and a bright pink polo shirt and she gave us a rather disinterested once-over. It didn't seem like she was dying to meet us.

"This is Ellie," explained Annabelle, beaming at us.

"And this is Grace," said another, much larger woman, emerging from the gloom with a girl who was her in miniature. Grace had very fine, very blond shoulder-length hair, a strand of which snaked into her mouth. Totally not dying to meet us, too.

"Don't do that, Grace," the woman said. "Honestly," she said to no one, or possibly everyone, "she's always sucking on her hair."

Grace didn't say anything as her mouth was full. We supposed the woman was her mother.

"Have you got your own ponies?" Ellie asked, flicking her long hair back behind her shoulders. Her very blue eyes peered out from under her bangs like two cornflowers under a hedge.

"Yes," I gulped, remembering my wonderful (albeit rose-tinted) Drummer and wishing he was with me. "Drum's a bay, all over, no white on him whatsoever. Look, I've got a picture of him on my phone." I found my favorite photo of Drum with his ears forward, smiling for the camera.

"He looks very nice," Grace said shyly.

Her mom peered over her shoulder to take a look. "Part Arab," she snapped, matter-of-factly. I nodded.

"And this is Tiffany," said Bean, wielding her phone like a light saber. "She's a bit nervous, but she's got a heart to match her color."

Ellie looked blank.

"Gold," Bean explained.

"I'm getting a pony, soon. A show jumper," Ellie told us.

"Fantastic!" I said. I mean, what's more exciting?

"Have you got a pony, Grace?" asked Bean.

Grace didn't get a chance to answer—her mother swooped in like a hawk.

"Not yet. Grace rides at the riding school presently, don't you Grace?" Before Grace had the chance to speak her mother continued, shaking her head, "I'm hoping this vacation will improve her confidence and get her going a bit. Honestly, when I was her age I was galloping about and leaping on and off ponies all day. Grace doesn't take after me, that's for sure!"

Grace just stood there, sucking her hair—probably grateful she didn't take after her mother. I felt sorry for her. What was her mother still doing here? I'd have died if my mom had come and hung around, voicing her disappointment with me to anyone within earshot. Annabelle seemed to feel the same way.

"Well, Mrs. Sharpe, I'm sure you have a long drive home, and you can see that Grace is fine with us. We'll take good care of her, won't we girls?"

"Hiya!"

We turned to see a girl with long, reddish blond hair, lots of black mascara and pink lip gloss climbing over the gate. Behind her, another girl tried to open the catch, her short, curly blond hair wobbling as she struggled.

"I'm Amber!" exclaimed the climber, leaping down and trotting toward us with a grin. "And this, if she ever gets here, is my sister Zoe."

We introduced ourselves—Grace's mother introduced Grace, adding that her daughter was a bit shy and she didn't know where she got it from.

No one else knew either.

Amber continued to grin at us. She and Zoe were a couple of years older than me and Bean, and looked fun.

"We'd rather you went *through* the gate, dear, instead

of over it," said Annabelle, smiling away like a ballroom dancer. "It's awfully bad for it."

"Told you!" said Zoe, scowling at her sister. "Unless you climb at the hinge end, it makes the gate drop."

"Oh, why do you always have to be right all the time?" moaned Amber, her shoulders sagging.

"You never pay attention, we've been told about gates before," Zoe said huffily.

Amber blew a defiant raspberry. "Phew," she said, running her fingers through her hair, "all this fuss over a gate! Have we met before?" she asked, looking at me quizzically. "Only you look really familiar."

I shook my head. I couldn't help thinking how Amber was the perfect name for her—her hair was the color of petrified tree resin. I would have remembered meeting someone as striking as her, I was sure.

"Come and have some refreshments," offered Annabelle, and we all followed her into the chill-out room where drinks were set out on a table. A big, black, fluffy cat sat on one of the three sofas, pony posters adorned the walls and there were horsey books and magazines scattered all around. I had hoped there'd be some food, I was starving!

"Cool place!" exclaimed Amber, reaching for a Coke.

"Have you got a pony?" Ellie asked her.

"No, worst luck!" Zoe interrupted, stroking the cat. "It's our dream to get one—maybe one day."

"I'm getting one—a show jumper," said Ellie. "I expect I'll win lots of ribbons and cups on mine."

"I'm sure you will, dear," soothed Annabelle, still smiling.

"I just want a pony to love, I don't care about winning stuff," Amber said bluntly, shrugging her shoulders. "I really want a chestnut with four white legs."

"Oh no, Amber, you know I want a dun," moaned Zoe, tickling the cat under the chin. The cat purred like a coffee-grinder and Annabelle told us he was called Soot.

"You could do with being a bit more ambitious, Grace," said her mother, giving her a poke. Grace's lack of reaction suggested poking was normal behavior.

"Now you're all here I can tell you about the fun we'll be having during the next five days," said Annabelle, her voice revving up to sound more exciting. "Ahhh, here's Sharon, our groom," she added, as a girl of about eighteen came bounding into the room. Slender with short, almost-white blond hair which stuck up in all directions like an explosion, Sharon wore a lemon polo shirt like Annabelle's (only dirtier), navy jodhpurs, chaps and dusty boots. It was obvious that Sharon did all the dirty work, leaving Annabelle to stay clean and stylish. She gave us a huge grin and winked. We all grinned back.

"Hi there!" she said. She looked a lot more fun than uptight Annabelle.

"I'm just about to run through the itinerary," Annabelle explained, waving her clipboard in the air.

"It's like prison camp, here," Sharon joked, winking at us. "You won't know what's hit you!"

Amber laughed, but Grace looked terrified.

"No it isn't, Sharon, everyone will have a wonderful time!" exclaimed Annabelle, clearly annoyed by Sharon's irreverence. "After lunch, I'll introduce you to the ponies. We've already allocated them to you all, according to the rider profiles you returned to us, but we may have to swap you round if we find things don't work out."

"Oh, who have I got?" pleaded Amber. "I so want Sorrel!"

"Only because you think she'll teach you the finer points of horsemanship," teased Zoe, quoting from the High Grove website.

"Get lost Zoe, you loser!" replied her sister.

Annabelle glanced at her clipboard, shook her head and looked a bit smug. "Sorry, my dears, no one will know until after lunch. We'll have a lesson this afternoon to make sure you all get on with your ponies, then after we've cleaned our tack and turned the ponies out, it's probably warm enough for a swim before supper. Then tonight we've got some wonderful horsey DVDs for you all to watch! Meanwhile, there's a full schedule on the notice board in the dining room. You'll also see there that we always have a best-kept pony competition, a tidiest-stable competition and a cleanest tack competition, so bear that in mind whenever you're grooming, mucking out and cleaning tack!"

I heard Bean groan. She hated doing any of those things. I thought Sharon could be right about the prison camp, despite the wink and the grin.

"Cool!" exclaimed Amber, punching the air. "I am so going to try to win one of those!"

"Same here!" said Ellie.

"You so won't, Amber," Zoe said. "You're always in too much of a hurry."

Amber pulled a face. "I said I'm going to try," she said. "There's nothing wrong with trying."

I heard Grace's mother whispering to Grace that she ought to try and win something. It would do her good, according to her mother. Grace stayed mute.

"Do you think Grace's mom is going to stay all week?" Bean whispered to me out of the corner of her mouth.

"Don't—that's totally not funny!" I whispered back, fighting visions of Grace's mom laden down with trophies—she'd be bound to win everything.

"I can't wait to tell Dee about her," Bean continued, staring at Grace's mom in fascinated horror. "She thinks her mom's bad!"

I nodded in agreement. Dee's mom Sophie was a hundred times better.

Finally, Grace's mother managed to tear herself away—but not before she'd had a long conversation with Annabelle, which we all overheard, regarding the expectations she had of High Grove Farm. It seemed that unless Grace morphed into a potential for the Olympic equestrian team over the next five days, she would consider the money paid for Grace's vacation totally down the drain.

"Your mom's a nightmare!" Amber said, nudging Grace's arm good-naturedly. "But most moms are!" she laughed.

For one horrified moment, I thought Grace was going to cry. Amber noticed, too.

"Hey, only joking! She's gone now, you've got five days of freedom!"

"She wants me to learn to jump," whispered Grace, frantically stroking Soot who, quite content in his role as comforter, closed his eyes and purred even louder. "But I don't want to. I just want to ride Bobbin, my favorite pony at my riding school, but she keeps on talking about getting me a pony."

"Why wouldn't you want to learn to jump?" sneered Ellie. "It's so totally the best thing. I could jump and jump and jump, it's so fantastic."

"Well, not everyone likes doing the same thing," said Bean. "If you don't want to jump, Grace, just say so."

Grace's blue eyes widened, her hand hovering over Soot in mid-stroke. "Can I do that?" she asked.

"Sure can!" said Amber. "If you can't, we'll stick up for you!"

"Why do you always have to shove your nose in, Amber?" asked Zoe. "It's none of your business."

"Hey, Grace is worried, I'm being supportive!" Amber said. "We have to stick up for each other, right?"

"Amber's right," said Bean passionately. "Grace is here to enjoy herself, not be scared into doing something she doesn't want to do. And I'm sure you'll get a fantastic pony, they all looked awesome on the website."

"I'm sure none of us will be made to do anything we don't want to," said Zoe. "We're on vacation, not at school."

"Well, I still don't see why you wouldn't want to jump!" said Ellie.

Bean put her arm round Grace. "Stop worrying. You're going to get a great pony and we'll all make sure you have a fantastic time!"

Grace nodded gratefully and resumed her cat-stroking offensive.

I could tell that Bean's sympathy with Grace was due to being so out of sync with her own family. Bean loved Tiffany and she rode really well. Her talents lay in other directions from the rest of her family and I wondered whether Grace was the same. Maybe she didn't want to ride. I couldn't help thinking that if that were true then Grace wasn't going to have a very good time on a riding vacation.

Not a good time at all.

CHAPTER 4

THE HIGH GROVE FARM ponies lined up along the fence, giving us the once-over and looking just as cute and awesome as they had on the website. I felt a shiver of excitement run through me. Never mind that Grace was nervous, I hadn't ridden any pony other than Drummer for ages. Curling my fingers around Epona in my pocket, I realized how much I was looking forward to enjoying some cozy chats with my allocated pony. Wouldn't he or she be surprised!

But then the effect of Epona kicked in and I could hear the ponies. I never learn…

"Will ya look at this group, what a bunch of amateurs!" exclaimed the piebald, Harry, looking us up and down through his long, white forelock. He spoke with a loud, confident, New York accent.

"I bet none of them can ride," sneered Sorrel, the chestnut. Her mane, by contrast, was pulled short and her legs, unlike Harry's, were sleek and free from feather. Her voice was clipped and uptight, like someone trying to talk fancy. "I bet I get another rider hanging on to my reins all week. I don't know what they teach people at riding schools these day, I really don't."

My initial thrill of anticipation tumbled down a notch.

"I don't care who I get, as long as it's not the fat one," whined Cherokee, the bay with white splashes, eyeing up Grace. "My legs won't stand the weight." I looked at his legs—white from the knees down, complimented by a splash of white on his nearside shoulder and another one on his offside flank, which broke up his dark brown body and black mane and tail. He looked so cool. He sounded anything but.

"Which one is the fat one?" asked Appaloosa Dot-2-Dot, her head going from side to side as she examined us all.

"I wouldn't worry," Harry told her. "She's obviously a Shadow candidate."

"What's that?" Upon hearing his name the ancient snowy-white pony opened his eyes briefly before closing them again.

"Don't worry, Shad, we'll wake you if anything interesting happens," promised Sprout, yawning.

"Which it won't!" snapped Sorrel.

Any enthusiasm I'd felt was now oozing out through my boots and trickling on to the grass like a mutating virus. This was so not what I'd expected.

"Which one is the fat one?" repeated Dot.

"Hey you guys, what does Dot-2-Dot have in common with my manger two minutes after feeding time?" asked Harry.

"They're both empty!" chorused the other ponies, laughing.

"I don't get that," said Dot.

"Are they saying anything?" Bean asked me, out of the side of her mouth. "Are they as cute as they looked on the website?"

"Yes they are," I hissed back, "and no they're not!"

"What do you mean?"

I sighed—I was about to burst Bean's bubble of positivity. "The piebald thinks we all look useless, Sorrel is uptight and grumpy and Cherokee keeps complaining about his legs—and they're being really rude about Grace."

"Grace? Why?"

"They say she's fat!"

Bean looked across at Grace who was sucking another strand of hair. "You couldn't call her fat," she murmured, "she's just a bit bigger than the rest of us."

"That's not how they see it."

Annabelle gave us all one of her trying-too-hard smiles. She had changed into a lavender-colored polo shirt with purple jodhpurs, which reminded me of Katy. I wondered, with a pang of homesickness, how she was getting on with Drummer and resolved to call her as soon as possible for an update.

Unaware of having lost me to thoughts of home, Annabelle continued, brandishing her clipboard. "We've allocated ponies according to your experience so now's your time to start bonding!"

Sharon held a green halter at arm's length. "Who's got Harry?" she asked Annabelle.

"Ellie, dear, we've given you Harry, our gorgeous pie-bald," Annabelle enthused. "I know you two are going to get on famously."

"Yeah, like a house on fire!" I heard Harry chuckle.

Taking the halter, Ellie glanced at the field gate, the confidence she'd shown earlier totally gone.

"We'll all go in and catch the ponies together," explained Annabelle.

"Shadow?" asked Sharon.

"Grace," said Annabelle.

"Phew!" sighed Bean.

"Thank goodness!" sighed Sorrel, as Grace took the blue halter from Sharon's outstretched hand.

"Told ya!" snapped Harry, triumphantly. "Saw that one coming a mile away!"

"Sprout?" asked Sharon, holding out a leather halter and rope. Annabelle read out my name. I had really wanted Cherokee, as he reminded me of Drummer, but Sprout looked fun, and I wasn't disappointed.

"He's a bit of a lunatic," Sharon told me, and winked.

"Oh, OK," I gulped, wondering what form of lunatic Sprout would be.

Amber got her wish and was paired with Sorrel, giving an air punch and emitting a yell of YES!, and Bean was given Cherokee ("Dirt-colored, thank goodness!" I heard her exclaim), which left Zoe to catch Dot-2-Dot with the pink harness presented to her by Sharon.

Accepting my carrot bribe, Sprout stuck his nose in his

harness without a murmur. His tiny pink snip was dead cute and his mane stuck up and wafted about as he moved, which made him look slightly manic. Stroking his nose I eyed him up and down. Bigger than Drummer—about 14.2 hands, whereas Drum is just over 14 hands—and slender in build, he looked part Welsh with a nice head and only a hint of feather on his heels. Bean caught Cherokee without any trouble, but Sharon had to help Grace with Shadow—even though he stood rooted to the ground like he was nailed there—and Annabelle fussed a bit around Ellie, but eventually we all had our ponies in their stables and were grooming them for our first ride.

"What's yours like?" I heard Harry yell to Sorrel. "I'm going to have to nurse mine all week if this is the best she can do."

"Mine's surprisingly competent," Sorrel snapped back about Amber. "Oh, wait a minute, I spoke too soon. Don't do it like that! All wrong—totally the wrong brush for totally the wrong place. Ouch! Honestly!"

"There's a spider on my harness," said Dot in a far-away, singsong voice.

"Shake it off quick, Empty!" advised Harry. "Otherwise we'll all suffer from their hysterics!"

"Mine seems to know what she's doing," I heard Cherokee say about Bean, "so that's one thing I won't have to worry about!" I was beginning to dread learning how Sprout viewed me. I made a special effort to be gentle as I groomed his face.

"Well, I've had better," I heard Sprout remark. The nerve! I was just deciding that I'd show him, when Zoe let out a blood-curdling shriek which made every equine head shoot upward in anticipation of, at the very least, a nuclear attack.

"Ouch, my ears!" I heard Cherokee groan. "Not to mention my nerves, which are now in shreds."

"Told ya, didn't I!" snapped Harry.

"You're such a know-all, Haz," said Sprout.

After Zoe had stopped hyperventilating at Dot's spider, and Amber had stopped laughing at her sister's dismay, and Zoe had stopped glaring daggers at Amber, we tacked up.

Stroking Sprout's neck I whispered in his ear, which flicked back at the sound of my voice. "What kind of lunatic are you?" I asked him as butterflies fluttered around in my stomach. Would I be able to cope with Sprout? Or would I embarrass myself in front of everyone? It was time to find out.

38

CHAPTER 5

EVERYONE TOOK AGES TO get their ponies ready but eventually we were in the outdoor school, mounted and lined up in front of Annabelle. Bean steered Cherokee up beside me.

"Cherokee feels so different to Tiffany," said Bean.

"You really suit him," I told her. "You're just the right size for him and your brown jodhpurs tone in with his color—and your new brown gloves do, too. You'd easily win a class for rider most like her pony."

"It's so funny seeing you on a different pony," said Bean. "What's Sprout like?"

"Not sure yet," I said, "but he's a lot narrower than Drum. I didn't realize what a tub Drum is!"

After Annabelle and Sharon had inspected our tack (Harry's green saddle blanket was all bunched up on the offside, which earned Ellie a black mark), and Annabelle had written some notes on her clipboard, we were ready to head out.

"OK, we'll all walk round in open order, so you can get used to your ponies, and then we'll go into closed order and see how you get on. Pia, dear, take leading file on the right rein, please."

I gave Sprout's sides a nudge with my legs, just as I would have done if I'd been on Drummer and he leapt into action, almost leaving me behind. Talk about an over-reaction! I'd have to tone down my leg aids—Sprout was obviously quite sensitive. My mount had a short, choppy stride, which made me feel like we were covering the ground at a super-fast rate. He carried his head high in front of my hands and I could see his mane going in all directions. Everything felt strange as we scuttled around the perimeter of the school and I felt very high up. Sprout's saddle was harder than Drummer's and his reins were narrow, which gave me a completely different feel on them. It felt so odd riding a different pony, plus—I realized with an apprehensive pang—I hadn't had a lesson for, like, centuries.

"Pia, my dear, see whether you can slow Sprout down with some half-halts," Annabelle suggested.

Half-halts, mmmm, I thought. Drum and I were so used to each other, we just sort of muddled along without thinking. Now I was on Sprout, I would have to wake up and remember how to ride. Straightening my back, I asked Sprout to slow down, releasing my aids as he responded. A half-halt. Or so I thought.

"You need to use your seat bones, Pia, dear," said Annabelle. "Apply your back brake, rather than just using the reins. Sit up. Taller, that's right. Now push your chest toward your hands—not too much, yes. Now can you feel your seat bones under you,?"

I could. And so could Sprout. He immediately slowed

down, which was a relief. I mean, no one likes being towed along by their mount, it's totally scary. With the brakes working I felt myself relax. Wow, I thought, this riding vacation could really help me brush up on my riding skills. Awesome!

Annabelle turned her attention to the others. Amber was to shorten her reins and sit up more, she was riding like a cowboy, apparently. Ellie was leaning forward and Annabelle told her to put her shoulders back and put more weight into her heels. Zoe, although her position was very good, needed to relax and allow her body to follow Dot's movement more. Annabelle then suggested that Grace remembered to breathe, instead of holding her breath in anticipation that something dreadful was going to happen—it wasn't, she assured her—and then she praised Bean's position and said that if she could remember to look up between Cherokee's ears, instead of down at the ground, she would be almost perfect. We were all instructed to remember what she'd said so she didn't have to keep saying it all week, which seemed fair enough. I was having great fun practicing my half-halts. Apparently, I was the only one.

"Here we go," I heard Sprout complain. "Usual thing— give them an idea that works and they do it to death. I'm going to be half-halting all week, I can see that!"

"At least mine's light. I don't fancy Shadow's job, carting Lumpy around all week!" laughed Harry.

I looked across at Grace on Shadow. She really wasn't

very big, and Shadow didn't seem bothered. Actually, Shadow seemed to be carrying out all the school movements without the need to stay awake!

As our lesson continued I got more used to Sprout and started to enjoy myself, although I was mortified to learn how sloppy my riding had become without regular lessons. Annabelle kept reminding me about my hands, my legs, my head—they were all doing something wrong. I'd been doing it badly for so long, the wrong things felt right so that when I corrected them, they then felt all wrong. I hoped by the end of the week that the feelings would be reversed and I would be a better rider. Wouldn't Drum be surprised!

I wasn't the only one having problems: Amber kept getting told to sit up—she did ride a bit slumped—and Zoe was rather wooden. Bean only needed a couple of tweaks, though, and she looked really tidy on Cherokee. It was odd seeing her on a different pony, I was so used to her on Tiffany. The surprise was Grace, who sat nicely and had Shadow doing everything right. After the criticism from her mother I'd expected her to be all over the place but she was a much better rider than Ellie, who was clearly a real novice. I couldn't help thinking that her boast about getting a show jumper was wildly optimistic.

We ended the lesson with the tiniest, weeniest jump. Annabelle explained that we'd be tackling small jumps and fallen logs out hacking and Bean and I exchanged glances—it sounded like fun to us! Unfortunately, it didn't to Grace, who looked like she was going to be sick. After some convincing Grace headed Shadow toward the pole, her eyes tightly shut. But the gray pony simply plodded over with the tiniest bunny hop. As she landed Grace, finding herself still in the saddle and in one piece, could have won the-biggest-grin-in-the-world competition. From that initial jump, poor Bobbin was history, replaced by Shadow as the new love of Grace's life!

Sprout's style was nothing like Shadow's. Launching himself at the jump five strides out like it was a high puissance wall at a show jumping competition, he neatly popped over it with a flick of his heels, leaving me ever-so-slightly behind, which Annabelle noticed. Sorrel copied Sprout's approach, then stopped dead at the last moment— exactly what Annabelle had told Amber to expect. Despite the warning, Amber slid over the chestnut mare's shoulder and onto the ground.

"Ouch!" she said.

"I'm so not into jumping," declared Sorrel, sticking her nose in the air in disdain.

"Ha, ha, ha, I can see Sorrel is helping you master the finer points of horsemanship already!" laughed Zoe.

Unhurt, Amber was up and in the saddle again in no time, a determined look on her face. Sorrel didn't get a chance to stop a second time—Amber kicked on and they sailed over the pole with room to spare.

"Well done, Amber!" said Annabelle. "You need to ride Sorrel like that when we're out, don't let her even think of stopping!"

"I'll think what I like, thank you!" said Sorrel, shaking her head in disgust.

By the end of the lesson the personalities of the ponies were becoming clearer. Harry was a loud joker, but kindly, taking care of Ellie. Short-tempered Sorrel huffed and puffed and complained all the time in her clipped tones. She wasn't taking any prisoners and it was clear Amber couldn't just sit there, she had to ride. Dot-2-Dot appeared to be in her own little bubble and didn't get what the others were saying most of the time, and the only thing I heard from Shadow was snoring. Cherokee was the whiner. If he wasn't complaining that his bridle pinched his ears he was telling everyone that his girth was too tight and that his legs weren't too good today. Sprout, I was still getting to know. Apart from going everywhere in a hurry he seemed fine, and once I got used to his stride I was sure I was going to enjoy riding him. My initial fears about not being able to cope melted away. Phew!

"That was really good!" enthused Annabelle, beaming at us as we lined up and dismounted. "Now we'll go in, feed and groom the ponies, and turn them out before cleaning tack."

Bean looked at me and rolled her eyes.

After untacking Sprout, I fetched his feed.

"Ah, at last!" he exclaimed, thrusting his nose into his manger and shoveling down his feed.

"Steady on," I said, patting his dappled neck and retreating. This was familiar ground—Drum loves food, too. As I bolted the door behind me, I noticed Grace hovering outside Shadow's door with the bucket as Shadow leaned over the door with an expectant look on his face. I had wondered what it would take to wake him up—a feed bucket seemed to do the trick.

"Help!" implored Grace.

"Just undo the door and tip the feed in his stall," I said.

"I can't," she whispered, "he looks wild!"

Wild? Jeez, she should see Drummer when he's kept waiting for his feed, I thought. Compared to dear old Shadow, he looked demented!

"Come on," I said, sliding the bolt open, "I'll come with you."

Pulling Grace in behind me, I showed her how to quickly upend the bucket in Shadow's stall and stand back. "Ponies are obsessed with food, Grace. The longer you keep them waiting, the worse they get. But look, Shadow won't hurt you, he's just greedy."

Grace stroked Shadow's snowy mane and bit her lip.

"I don't think I'll ever cope with a pony of my own," she said.

"Don't you want a pony?" I asked. I mean, who wouldn't?

"Oh, I'd love a pony like Shadow, but not one like my mom would want me to have."

I thought of the type of pony Grace's mom would buy—one like Tiffany, or Dolly, or a younger Sorrel. A pony that would satisfy Grace's mom would terrify Grace. She was a classic sufferer of OAP syndrome—over-ambitious-parent.

Tack cleaning was eventful: Bean did her usual hasty

wipe over with a soapy cloth. Zoe took Dot's bridle apart and spent ages poking saddle soap out of the holes with a stalk of straw and Amber copied Bean, telling jokes the whole time. Grace cleaned Shadow's tack carefully and thoroughly but Ellie used a sopping wet sponge, so Harry's bridle went all hard and dull. I hoped I'd done a decent job on Sprout's tack and it looked pretty good when I'd finished. But what I thought of it didn't count. Annabelle carried out an inspection—awarding points and scribbling notes on her clipboard.

We brushed the ponies over before turning them out. I sponged feed dust from Sprout's muzzle and picked out his hooves before brushing out his saddle mark.

"Oooo, that feels much better," he said.

"You're welcome," I said. He gave me a funny look. "I've got a pony called Drummer at home," I told him, wondering what Drum was doing. Was he out in the field with Bluey? Or finishing his feed and neighing for Katy to let him out?

Sprout was silent.

"Why do you call Dot-2-Dot 'Empty'?" I asked him.

"Because she is—totally empty, nothing going on in her head," he said. Then he turned his head very slowly, and stared at me. I could almost hear his brain working, wondering how I could possibly know Dot's nickname.

I nodded my head. "Yup, I can hear you," I said. "You, and Harry, and Sorrel. All of you. I'm totally fluent in pony-speak."

"Yeah, yeah, of course you are," Sprout muttered, to himself.

"Harry's very New York, Sorrel's full of herself and Cherokee has every complaint under the sun, it seems," I told him.

Sprout just stared at me, saying nothing.

"Go on," I challenged him, "tell me something I would never know."

"My mother's name was Spice," he said slowly.

"Spice," I said, "is a very nice name for a pony."

Sprout did a double-take. Then he stepped back and looked me up and down before shaking his head. "I don't think so. No, no, no, no, so not happening..."

"It so is," I said, nodding.

"Are you ready, Pia?" asked Annabelle, sticking her head over Sprout's half-door and bestowing a smile on me.

"Absolutely," I said and led my bemused pony out into the sunshine.

CHAPTER 6

OF COURSE, WITH SIX of us in the one room at the top of the house, we didn't go to sleep for ages. After turning out the ponies we'd all had a great time in the swimming pool before showering for dinner—pasta, pizza and salads, followed by apple crumble and fresh fruit. We were starving! Amber kept saying she was sure she knew me from somewhere, but I assured her she didn't. Amber wasn't the sort of person you could easily forget.

Katy had texted me during dinner. I'd been kept so busy I hadn't had a chance to call her—cell phones were banned on the yard. Drummer GR8, I read. Went riding 2day with James (ouch! I thought). Going 2 old Mill 2MRO with Cat. Hope UR having GR8 time. K.

I texted back: Good here. My pony called Sprout. Love & XXXs to Drum. P. I felt a pang of homesickness and thought of Drummer, out in the field with Bluey and the others. Was he missing me?

I hadn't had time to be homesick for long because after dinner we'd watched some fantastic DVDs of Badminton and the show jumping at Olympia, and Amber and Zoe managed to keep it down to a single fight about when they went to Olympia last year and which of them had asked

William Whitaker for his autograph. Amber insisted she'd approached him but Zoe said she'd been too chicken, and that it had been she who had plucked up the courage and got him to sign their programs.

"Who cares who asked whom for what?" Bean had said later.

"Not me," I'd replied. "Do you argue with your sisters like that?"

"No," Bean had said. "We rarely talk."

As we all lay in our beds under the rafters, we discovered that Ellie's favorite pony at her riding school was a gray Connemara called Eddie (on whom she could do shoulder-in and was hoping to do flying changes soon—which was an obvious fairy tale because no way could Ellie ride well enough to do those things), that Zoe hated cheese, that Grace's favorite thing to do was draw ponies and that Amber was missing her boyfriend, Ben, who, according to Zoe, was a complete geek. This gave the sisters another excuse to hurl insults at each other until Bean mentioned that she had won her vacation in a competition, which shut everyone up as they all wanted to know more. I got a big credit but I wasn't really listening. I was thinking of Amber missing Ben, and wondering whether James, whose pony Moth lives next to Drummer, and is knee-meltingly adorable, was missing me. I wouldn't have minded being able to tell everyone that he was something more than a friend, but no such luck. Then it occurred to me that he might have sent me a text, especially as he is the only other person who knows my pony-whispering talents depend on Epona, which gives us the merest hint of an excuse for a special relationship—at least, I like to imagine so.

I wriggled down under the duvet and switched on my cell phone again, but of course, no text from James.

"What are you doing under there?" asked Amber.

"Nothing, just checking my messages," I told her, innocently. Then I remembered that she and Zoe hadn't seen my photo of Drum, so I scrolled through again and showed Amber.

"Oh, he's so cute!" she said, grabbing my phone and before I could stop her she scrolled through all my other photos. "Here's Bean on a palomino at a show…and another one of Drum in the field…and who's this?" She turned my mobile round to show me—and everyone else. "He's cute!" she cried, giving me a wide-eyed, knowing look.

I could have died. She'd found the photo of James with Moth I'd taken at the yard. I had photos of Katy and Bluey and Dee and Dolly, too, but of course, it would be the one of James Amber focused on.

"That's James," said Bean in a bored voice. "And that's Moth. Did you see the one of me on Tiff? Isn't she just the coolest?"

I held my breath. Bean being so dismissive about James had helped me out. Amber wasn't going to let it go, though.

"He's adorable!" she exclaimed, examining the photo again. "Look, Zo, isn't he just too cute? You're so lucky, we've got absolutely no good-looking boys at our riding school, do we, Zo?"

"No, not one," Zoe said, pulling a face. At last, something they agreed on, I thought.

Amber threw me back my phone. "Do us a favor and send that picture on to me, will you?" she said. "I'll show Ben and tell him James was here for the week. That'll get him going!"

"You're totally pathetic, Amber!" her sister told her.

"You're the pathetic one!" her sister snapped back. "It's not like you've got a boyfriend, and—duh—Patrick Williams is never, ever going to ask you out!"

"Oh shut up!" yelled back Zoe.

"I'm just going to send a text," I said, disappearing under the duvet with my phone again in case I'd turned red.

"To James?" teased Amber.

"To my mom, actually!" I yelled from my cocoon. So I did, sending her a picture of Sprout I'd taken on my phone, and telling her about him. I thought about texting James, but Amber had made me feel weird about it.

When I stuck my head out over the duvet again, everyone was talking about their ponies.

"I'm glad Harry can jump," said Ellie, "because I have to practice this week for when I get my show jumping pony."

"I don't," mumbled Grace.

"What is that you've got in bed with you, Grace?" asked Ellie, leaning over and tweaking the duvet.

"Nothing!" lied Grace.

"It's a toy pony. How babyish!" Ellie sneered.

"Let us see, Grace," Zoe said. "I love ponies figurines, I've got hundreds of them."

"I've got some, too," volunteered Bean. "Which one have you got there?"

"It's Major, my favorite," said Grace, holding up a small, plastic black pony.

"You'll like Silver, look," said Amber, showing her a thin, leather rope on which swung a glittering, galloping silver pony.

"Oh, he's gorgeous," breathed Grace.

"Yeah, he's my good luck charm," said Amber, returning the necklace to the table beside her.

"Major's cool! He's a Breyer, isn't he?" asked Bean. Grace nodded.

"Toy ponies?" retorted Ellie. "I grew out of them years ago."

"Some of them are collectable—adults collect them, actually, so that's all you know, Miss Know-it-all." Amber pulled a face at Ellie and Ellie turned bright pink. "Our grandma collects figurines—they go for hundreds of dollars at auction."

"Our mom keeps saying they're her inheritance," Zoe laughed. "I hope they're worth millions 'cause they'll be our inheritance, too!"

"My mom says we're going to inherit a place in Spain from Granddad," said Grace.

"Your mom's very forceful, isn't she?" said Zoe. "It's

like she wants a pony more than you do. Why doesn't she just get herself a horse?"

"I don't know," sniffed Grace. "But I wouldn't mind a pony if it was like Shadow. What's your mom like, Bean?"

"She's a sculptor," said Bean.

"Wow, how exciting!" Amber exclaimed, bouncing up and down. "Is she famous?"

"Yeah, unfortunately," said Bean in a bored voice.

"My mom's dating," I said. "Which, I have to tell you, is a nightmare!"

"I wish my mom would date someone," said Grace. "Since she and Dad split up, she's gone back to horses in a big way. If she had a boyfriend, it might get her off my case."

I wondered what sort of boyfriend Grace's mom would attract. It wasn't a pretty picture, imagining her mom on a date. She'd probably tell the poor man what he was going to eat and drink, and straighten his tie. If his hair was long enough, he'd start sucking on it within the first twenty minutes.

Looking round at everyone I noticed that Ellie had gone uncharacteristically quiet and was biting her nails. Amber suddenly seemed to notice, too.

"OK, Ellie, we've dished the dirt on our moms, tell us what yours is like," she said.

Suddenly, there was a bang on the door and Mrs. Reeve's voice called out. "Girls, come on now, go to sleep. It's late and you've got a full day tomorrow!"

Everyone went quiet. Then, hearing Mrs. Reeve's

footsteps recede, we started giggling. From then on, we spoke in whispers until gradually, one by one, the whispers stopped as everyone around me fell asleep. Someone snored—I think it was Zoe.

I was tired and could feel my eyes closing. I wondered what we would do tomorrow, and how Sprout was going to react after my revelation today. And then, just as I was dropping off, I thought I could hear the faint sound of someone crying. It had to be Grace, I thought, worrying about the pony her mom threatened to buy her. When I got Drummer I remember it being the best day of my life ever, EVER. Poor Grace ought to be excited, not scared, I thought. But then I remembered—the chosen pony would have to satisfy the mother, not Grace. No wonder she was scared.

CHAPTER 7

WHEN ARE YOU GOING to talk to Cherokee and tell me what he's like?" asked Bean.

"I've told you what he's like," I replied. "He's a total hypochondriac and keeps whining about his legs. He also says his bridle's too tight and complains that it squeezes his ears."

"You're exaggerating!" exclaimed Bean. "He's so cute!"

I sighed. My pony-whispering had got me into trouble before when I'd told owners what their ponies had said, things they hadn't wanted to hear. I didn't want to go down that road with Bean.

"Well, check out his bridle, then," I told her, shrugging my shoulders.

She did. It fit fine, she replied.

"See?" I said, vindicated. "Hypochondriac—he loves imagining he's ill!"

"Are you absolutely sure?"

"I don't make these things up, you know," I told her. "Oh, and we have to be nice to poor Grace, I heard her crying last night."

"Crying?" said Bean, looking over at Grace. "I *am* nice to her."

"Yes, you are, really nice, actually," I conceded. "I think she's really worried about the sort of pony her mom might buy her."

"Poor Grace," said Bean. "How awful it must be to be scared of what you most love doing. I suppose we forget what that's like because we're lucky enough to have our own ponies. If we only rode once a week at a riding school we'd have a whole week to forget what we'd learned last week, and worry about what we were going to do the next week. I mean, in a lesson, you have to do what the instructor tells you, but we can do what we like."

Bean was right, we were incredibly lucky. I felt another homesick pang for Drummer. What would he be doing now—grazing with his beloved Bambi? Chatting with his friend Bluey? Trying to get away from Dolly's incessant chatter?

Sprout had looked at me suspiciously as I'd led him in from the field. I'd ruffled his mad mane and told him I knew he didn't believe I could hear him, but assured him that it was true. He'd said nothing. Either he was in denial (I knew how that felt!), or he wasn't chancing it. The other ponies weren't so restrained.

"Will you go easy with the dandy brush!" I heard Sorrel exclaim. "Some of us have sensitive, thoroughbred skin!"

"I think I'm getting a cough" mumbled Cherokee as Bean tightened up his girth.

"This morning, girls, we are going for a ride," declared Annabelle, looking particularly fruit-like in a strawberry-colored top and green jodhpurs. A cheer went up. We were all dying to explore the countryside.

With Annabelle mounted on a big iron gray Warmblood called Tailor, and Sharon on her own cheeky-looking liver chestnut Arab mare with a white blaze, called Caramel, we all trooped out of the yard and along a sandy track before turning into a pine forest, with Amber and Zoe arguing about which of them should be in front of the other. The countryside was totally different than where I ride Drum. Our forests are mostly deciduous trees, which lose their leaves in winter, and the ground is mostly clay so it gets all boggy in winter, and bakes hard in summer. The soil around High Grove Farm was soft sand that the ponies kicked up in clouds, and we were soon covered in a fine film of yellow dust. Now and again, the ponies sneezed to clear their noses of it and it wasn't long before I found myself sneezing, too. Between clumps of pine trees we rode out across a field dotted with yellow gorse bushes. The sky was clear and there was only a slight breeze—it was totally perfect riding weather.

Away from the confines of the school Sprout jogged sideways, his mane wafting in the breeze as he bobbed along, swinging his bottom into Cherokee.

"Careful Sprout, you almost stepped on me—that's all my legs need!" complained Bean's tricolored pony. "I don't know why the management doesn't fit me with overreach boots, it knows I'm a slave to my bad legs."

"What's he saying?" asked Bean. "Come on, Pia, don't be mean."

"He's whining about his legs," I told her, feeling a bit sick due to Sprout's persistent jogging. It was like riding a pony on a boat in high seas.

"He must be saying more than just that!" Bean exclaimed.

I shook my head. "He isn't, he just rattles on all the time about his legs, his back, the cough he thinks he's getting," I told her in a loud whisper. I couldn't risk anyone else hearing me. I thought Drum complained a lot, but Cherokee was like a squeaky door in a high wind by comparison.

Bean didn't believe me. Pulling a face, she dropped back to ride with Amber who was once again riding like a cowboy, much to Sorrel's disgust.

"Lazy riding," I heard her mutter. "Disgraceful!"

"I told you Sprout was a nut-case, didn't I?" Sharon said, urging Caramel up beside me. "Just go all floppy on him, like a rag doll," she advised, her hair poking out under her riding hat like it was trying to make a getaway. Her clothes were still grubby. It was Sharon who tidied up the yard and made sure the tack room was in order, filled the water trough in the field, dished out feeds and humped hay and straw around. Annabelle sort of swanned about, making sure we did everything correctly while Sharon worked. I suppose overseeing six young riders with ponies was work, but it wasn't work that got you dirty, that was for sure.

I did as Sharon suggested and as I went into rag doll mode Sprout broke into a walk, accompanied by a sigh of relief.

"He'll teach you loads, that pony will," said Sharon, giving me a wink. "You're going to get along fine."

I couldn't help thinking she was right. I was learning a lot on Sprout.

We had a great ride. The sandy paths were perfect for long canters, and the ponies seemed to enjoy it much more than they had yesterday's lesson. Cherokee complained about sand going up his nose and Sorrel whined when she had to walk at the back—she seemed to think she ought to lead—but apart from that, everyone seemed to enjoy themselves. Even Grace had a huge smile on her face as Shadow chugged along at whatever pace she wanted him to—which was about a mile a week. He really was perfect for her. I noticed that Bean steered Cherokee over to ride next to her for a while, talking to her and helping her out when Sharon, who had been doing the same thing, was distracted by questions from other riders.

Sprout kept annoyingly quiet. I patted his neck and chatted away to him but he wasn't having any of it. Until we all stopped for a break. Dismounting, we loosened our girths and munched on fruit and granola bars Sharon produced from her backpack. Sprout kept giving me sly, sideways glances.

"I'm bored. I vote we liven things up on the way home," said Harry, pulling a protesting Ellie across the clearing and tugging at a tasty branch.

"Oh yes, let's do something," agreed Sorrel. "We can start a mock fight, that always gets them going. I bet Shadow's rider is a squealer."

"As long as she doesn't do it too loudly," said Cherokee. "My ears won't stand it."

"What's a squealer?" asked Dot, lifting her nose and crossing her eyes to look at a fly on her noseband.

"Shhhh," said Sprout.

"What's your problem?" asked Harry, stopping in mid-munch. "It's not like they can hear us."

"*She* can," said Sprout, jerking his head toward me.

"She can what?" asked Dot.

"You've lost it, man," laughed Harry. "They'll be carting you off to a retirement farm if you don't pull yourself together!"

"No, I haven't, she can hear us. I don't know how, but she can. Ask her to repeat something you've said. Go on, find out for yourself," said Sprout, stamping his near fore, annoyed that none of his friends believed him.

"OK then, if she can hear us, perhaps she'll be good enough to let us know what she thinks of our mock fight plans, ha, ha!" laughed Harry, returning his attention to the leafy twig.

"I don't think a mock fight is a good idea," I said quietly. All the ponies turned to stare at me—even Shadow opened his eyes for that. Harry paused in mid-munch.

"Who said anything about a fight?" said Amber, frowning.

"What are you on about?" asked Ellie.

Harry spat out a half-eaten leaf and gulped. "Wow, Sprout, you were right! She *can* hear us. How does she do that?"

"No idea," snapped Sprout.

"Nightmare!" exclaimed Sorrel. "I mean, imagine that happening in the show ring. Dis-aaaaa-ster!"

"What's the problem?" asked Dot. "I think it's sweet."

"Oh, Empty, get up to speed!" sighed Cherokee.

"Pia, sweetie," said Annabelle, over-brightly, "what's this about a fight?"

I turned my attention from the ponies to Annabelle. Another tricky little situation to get myself out of. Engage brain, Pia, if you can locate it!

"Er, well, Bean and I are part of a re-enactment group at school. We don't really fight. We were just talking about it." I could see Bean's puzzled expression, but she didn't say anything. She's used to my pathetic attempts to worm my way out of situations my pony-whispering shoves me into.

Satisfied, Annabelle went back to trying to prevent Tailor from grazing. As he was at least 16.2 hands and built like a multi-story parking garage, it took all her attention.

"Tell Cherokee I think he's really cool," said Bean, offering the tricolored pony a mint. So I did, even though he could hear Bean perfectly well. Cherokee didn't return the compliment. Instead, he muttered something about preferring apples as they were better for his teeth. He then went into one about a friend of his who had choked on a mint and had spent the night in the veterinary hospital yadda yadda yadda. I switched off after the first few minutes.

Mounting up, we went for another ride around the forest. On the way home, Annabelle told us we were going over some teeny-weeny jumps, which caused Grace to go apoplectic until Sharon said she would stay at the back with her and take it really slowly, assuring her that she *could* go around the jumps if she really wanted to. The rest of us were up for it.

"Race you!" challenged Amber, revving up Sorrel with her legs and holding her with the reins. Sorrel started doing half-rears on the spot.

"No racing!" Annabelle said firmly. "Single file, in an orderly fashion, please. I don't want to take back a group of broken riders and ponies."

"Buzz kill!" whispered Amber.

"And remember, Amber," added Annabelle, looking around, "Sorrel may try to duck out or refuse again, so leg on."

"I'll be fine!" Amber said breezily. "I've got the measure of her now!"

The jumps were only tiny, but the ponies charged toward them in excitement—especially Sorrel who had been thoroughly wound up by Amber by the time we reached them. Amber thought it was hilarious but Zoe went all sister-ish and started saying she was acting immaturely—probably because Dot, who was really young, started to plunge about in excitement. Except that Dot cleared each jump and shot off after Tailor whereas Sorrel, who was in front of me and Sprout, put in a spectacular stop at the first, tiny log—barely a twig. Amber slid down her neck and landed in the dust with a thud. I heard Sprout snort with disgust, muttering, "Oh no, not again! Every single time!" with a sigh.

"What did I tell you, Amber?" asked Annabelle, cantering back. "Are you all right?"

Amber leapt up, grinned, dusted herself off and mounted the chestnut mare again. "I'll learn—eventually!" she laughed.

"Can't you stay in the saddle for five minutes?" yelled Zoe.

"For gawd's sake, Sorrel," I heard Harry shout from the back, "are you still messin' about with them jumps?"

"I don't do jumps, I'm a show pony!" said Sorrel indignantly.

"WAS," shouted Cherokee. "Now you're a riding vacation pony, and you need to get over it!"

"That's really funny coming from you, with all your fake illnesses!" huffed Sorrel. "Anyway, it's good for my riders, it teaches them to keep their knees in and ride me forward!" she added, defensively.

After cheerfully telling Zoe to put a sock in it, Amber put Sorrel at the log again and this time, she legged on like mad. Sorrel had nowhere to go but over it ("See, at least I teach my riders something," she shouted indignantly), and we were off again.

Ellie, despite her boastings about wanting to be a show jumper, almost fell off over the last jump and was only saved by Harry lifting his head and shoving her back in the saddle. Sprout just stuck his head in the air, cantered sideways and then charged at each jump, leaping far higher than he needed to—the jumps were only tiny, after all. There seemed to be a lot going on underneath me—Sprout lifted his knees up high and jiggled about, but because he didn't have the same weight as Drum, and was a more slender build, he was easy to keep seated on. I felt like my knees would meet in the middle, he was so narrow.

We all pulled up breathlessly at the end of the jumps and waited for Sharon and Grace to catch up with us.

"I bet Grace is wetting herself," sneered Ellie.

"No she's not, look!" I said.

Grace had the biggest grin on her face as Shadow carefully bounced over each jump. It was almost as though the gray pony was making it as comfortable as he could for his nervous rider. What a star, I thought. Sharon had Caramel matching him, stride for stride, and was encouraging Grace as she rode alongside.

Standing up in her stirrups, Amber circled the air with one hand and yelled, "Yea, Grace! Wow, she's better than me!"

"Oh, that was fantastic!" enthused Grace as Shadow came to a halt, his sides heaving, and she threw her arms around his neck. Shadow was already catching up on his zzzzzs.

"Well done Grace!" enthused Annabelle, with a smile.

We walked home. At least, everyone else did, Sprout jogged sideways, shaking his head and muttering to himself. I could barely make out what he was saying but he was obviously over-excited. I tried going rag dollish, but it didn't make any difference.

"I told you—lunatic!" said Sharon, shaking her head, which didn't seem terribly helpful but everyone likes to be proved right, I suppose.

Bean steered Cherokee up beside us and looked at Sprout. "He's got energy to spare," she remarked.

"You could say that," I replied. Then Sprout suddenly decided to walk and he fell in step with Cherokee, enthusiastically sneezing dust out of his nose.

"Not too close!" the tricolored said. "Consider the possible germ-transference!"

"Give it a rest," Sprout sighed.

"What do you think of Ellie?" Bean asked me in a hushed tone.

"Er, well, she doesn't really endear herself to anyone, does she?" I replied.

"She's been telling me all about how she's going to get a pony—again—and how it's going to be a top show jumper, but she's not much of a rider," remarked Bean. "I mean, I'd have thought she'd be better off with a quieter pony. She can't even ride as well as Grace."

"I agree. But if she wants to live in a fantasy world, let her. I never know how to take her: one minute she's all sneery and annoyingly stuck up, the next she's all quiet like she's somewhere else. It's almost like she's two different people—one of them can't wait to impress us, the other doesn't even want to talk to us."

"Amber and Zoe are totally crazy!" Bean giggled.

"You can say that again. I like them, though," I told her.

"Oh yes, so do I. And Grace, I like Grace, too. Her riding isn't as bad as she thinks, I wish she'd believe in herself a bit more."

"Would you, if you had her mom?" I said.

"Good point! You can see that she just makes Grace nervous and sucks all her confidence away. Shadow's perfect for her, isn't he? He's such a star!"

I looked ahead to where Grace was leaning down and stroking the gray's neck. "She loves him, it's a shame her mom can't buy Shadow."

"Why can't she?" said Bean, her eyes flashing. "We have to get her to buy him!"

"What?"

"We have to make her mom see that Shadow is perfect for Grace!" said Bean.

"I don't think we can make her mom do anything," I said doubtfully. I couldn't imagine even asking her very nicely for something, let alone trying to force her to do something. The idea made me shudder.

"Mmmm, I know what you mean," Bean said, slumping in the saddle. Cherokee gave a loud groan, followed by a lot of muttering.

"Besides, Shadow probably isn't for sale," I said. "And he's ancient. He might not like moving stables."

"Oh, I suppose so. But Grace so needs a pony like him," Bean said as we rode our ponies into the stable yard for more tack cleaning and another round of Annabelle's overzealous inspection, complete with obligatory clipboard.

After lunch (tuna and ham rolls, salad and yogurt), Annabelle gave us all a lecture on feeding. Did you know that if you were to stretch out a pony's intestines (so not a nice image!), they could be as long as sixty yards in length? Plus, a pony's stomach is only about the size of a football and it can't stretch, which is why we should give them small feeds more often, instead of fewer big meals? No, well, neither did I, but I do now.

I talked to Sprout as I brushed out the dried sweat from his coat.

"I'm not your enemy, honestly," I told him. "I don't want anyone else to know I can hear you, so I'm not going to mention it. I promise."

Sprout gave me a look—he seemed to be making up his mind. "OK," he said, "I believe you—I have to—but you must admit it's not normal."

"Oh, absolutely!" I agreed. "But like I say, I don't want everyone to know either."

"OK then, truce," offered Sprout. "Can you scratch the top of my tail, please? No, not there, higher, lower, that's it, just there…ahhhhh! Mmmm, I can see this could have advantages!"

"Can I ask you something?"

"Can't exactly stop you, can I?" Sprout replied.

"Do you think you could cut out the jogging?" I asked him. My fingernails filled up with grease from his coat as I dug them into his tail.

"Mmmm, that might be tricky," he said, closing his eyes in bliss. "But I'll make a note of it and see what I can do. It's my nerves, you see."

"Oh, I see," I said, not seeing at all.

67

Suddenly, I heard a commotion on the yard and we both stuck our heads out over Sprout's door to see what was going on. Amber was yelling at Zoe, and Zoe was yelling back. Again.

"You shouldn't wear it all the time!" Zoe yelled. "You know it's valuable!"

"What's the point of having it if I don't wear it?" Amber shouted back. "It would be like having a Porsche and taking the bus everywhere!"

"Well, you won't be wearing it any more, will you?" Zoe sneered.

"Whatever is the matter, girls?" asked Annabelle, giving them one of her specialty smiles-under-pressure.

Zoe pointed to her sister and narrowed her eyes. "Ask her!" she said.

Amber shrugged, "I've lost my silver pony charm," she said. "And it's worth a lot."

CHAPTER 8

"IT MUST HAVE FALLEN off when I was out riding this morning," Amber told Annabelle. "I need to go and look for it, it's valuable."

"Are you sure?" Annabelle asked her.

"Oh yes, it's antique, not some worthless piece of old junk," nodded Amber.

"No, I mean are you sure you lost it out riding?" asked Annabelle testily.

"Mmmm, I'm pretty sure," said Amber. "But I don't mind missing this afternoon's lesson and looking for it, honest."

"Sharon can go and look," said Annabelle. Sharon looked less than delighted.

As Sharon rather forcefully convinced Caramel that another ride was just what she needed, we all rode into the school for another lesson. I did a bit better this time— managing to get my half-halts half-right. Bean was getting on famously with Cherokee, she even got him thinking so much about his circles and his figure-eights, he forgot to whine about his ears/back/legs/mouth/you-name-it/pains/aches/terminal illness. My circles got better as my figure-eights improved, and Grace did some fantastic ones on

Shadow. Ellie's were more like spirals and her figure-eights were like two fat squares, and Zoe had trouble with Dot as she was really young and didn't have much of a clue about what was expected of her, but Amber and Sorrel did perfect circles every time. But then, as Sorrel pointed out to the other ponies, she used to do circles and figure-eights for a living in the show ring.

"I'm a professional!" she declared.

"Yeah, professional has-been!" laughed Harry.

"At least I wasn't in trade," snapped Sorrel.

"It was hard work," grumbled Harry. "You try pulling a cart around all day, six days a week. You'd never stand the pace."

"Neither did you!" mumbled Cherokee.

"My owner retired," explained Harry. "Nice old guy he was, very forthcoming with the carrots. Made an honest livin' and owed nuthin' to no one."

I couldn't help wondering how such a mix of ponies came to be at High Grove Farm. Perhaps they'd been cheap, or a group sold together. I mean, what were the chances? On the other hand, how did I know all stables didn't have such colorful characters?

We'd turned the ponies out and tidied the stables by the time Sharon and Caramel returned. Sharon shook her head. "I'm sorry, Amber, but I couldn't find it," she said, her face downcast.

"Oh no," wailed Amber, "I can't believe I've lost Silver. I won't have any luck, now."

"Mom's going to kill you!" declared Zoe. "She's always telling you not to wear it when you go riding."

"Oh, put a sock in it, Zoe. You're so bossy sometimes!" Amber shouted at her, and they had another fight which only stopped when Annabelle waded in.

"Are you absolutely sure you had it on when you went riding this morning?" Annabelle asked Amber.

Amber sighed. "I'm certain. I always put Silver on first thing in the morning."

"But you got up late this morning," said Zoe. "Are you sure you didn't forget 'cause you were in a hurry to go and get Sorrel saddled?"

Amber looked thoughtful. "I'll go and check my bedside table," she said, running upstairs. Sharon looked less than pleased at the possibility of having spent all that time looking for something which was upstairs, but Amber soon returned, looking crestfallen. "No Silver. I must have put him on this morning!"

Annabelle sighed. "In that case, we'll keep looking when we're out riding, but it doesn't seem very promising, does it?" She turned to all of us. "If anyone else has anything valuable with them, it might be a good idea to keep it safe upstairs, rather than risk losing it out riding."

My hand went immediately to Epona, safely stashed in my pocket, as always. There was no way I was storing her in my bag upstairs. My little stone statue of the Celtic goddess sitting sideways on her horse would go with me wherever I went.

Amber was amazingly philosophical about her lost lucky charm—she was soon laughing and splashing about in the swimming pool. Zoe seemed more upset that her sister had been so careless. Amber just shrugged her shoulders when I quizzed her about it.

"I'm really upset, actually," she said, "but what can I do about it? If Silver turns up, fantastic. If not…well, I'll have to find another lucky charm. He couldn't have been that hot as a lucky charm if he's managed to get himself lost, could he?"

"But I thought you said he was valuable?" I said.

"Yeah, he was. I'm not looking forward to telling my mom I've lost him—she bought him for me for my birthday. But then," she said, grinning at me, "I probably won't get a chance to—I bet Zoe's dying to tell her!"

That evening, Mom called me on my cell phone.

"How's it going," she asked me. "Are you having a fabulous time?"

I assured her I was and told her all about Sprout.

"How did he react when you started talking to him?" she asked. I told her he was still getting used to it. Then I asked her how she was and whether she'd been out anywhere nice.

"Oh, Pia, I'm very excited," she said. "I think this could be The One!"

"Which one, Leonard or Simon," I asked, trying unsuccessfully to conjure up an image of either of Mom's two suitors. Surely neither of them could be The One.

"Who?" asked Mom. "Oh no, Pia, Leonard's out of the running."

"Why?"

"He turned up on a date wearing those ugly '80s style shoes I hate."

I didn't know what she was going on about. When it came to men, Mom seemed to have a language all her own. Assuming then that Simon, by default, was The One, I asked where they'd been together.

"No, no, I've given Simon the old heave-ho, as well," Mom said.

"Why?" I asked, my brain getting more tangled by the second.

"Nose hair," came the reply. "No, I'm talking about Andy."

My mom is so superficial. Honestly, she's always telling me I have to see beyond what people look like and seek the inner person, find out whether they are kind, or considerate or have hidden qualities, blah, blah, blah (apart from Dad's girlfriend, Skinny Lynny—she can't stop thinking up snide comments about her). Then, as soon as one of her boyfriends wears the wrong shoes or she notices a hair sprouting in the wrong place, she dumps them. What chance do I have of having any sort of quality relationship with any future boyfriends with such a bad role model?

"Andy?" I asked faintly. There had been no mention of an Andy before I left. It was only two days ago, for heaven's sake.

"Yup! Andy is a lawyer," Mom said reverently.

"Is that good?" I asked, bewildered.

"Good? It's better than good. I'm telling you, Pia, Andy would have come in very handy when your father and I were going through our divorce."

Stable, door, bolted—all words which sprang to mind but instead of mentioning them out loud, I asked Mom about shoes, nasal sproutings, and other possible barriers to true love.

"Nope, Andy wears very stylish shoes. No nasal hair. No ear hair either. In fact," she paused, "Andy has no hair at all, head-wise."

"He's bald?"

"Yes, but it suits him and, as Carol says…"

I groaned inwardly. Her friend Carol's opinion is highly valued by my mom, highly dreaded by me.

"…bald is very fashionable. Very now."

"Well as long as you're having fun," I said, giving up.

I hung up and shared my concerns with Bean. She looked at me vacantly, unable to comprehend a parent with such an active social life. "At least your mom doesn't appear from her studio at eight o'clock at night, after everyone else has cooked their own dinner, and ask what you'd like for lunch," she said.

"Why don't you buy her a watch?" I asked.

"We did. Several," Bean replied. "They turned up fused together in a block of Plexiglas, titled *Time: Frozen*, and exhibited at the local museum. Some mental person actually bought it for a couple of thousand dollars. She uses everything in her sculptures. She stole some of my school pens for some piece she did about education. Honestly, you can't leave anything lying around."

Obviously, when one is artistic, one loses track of time or how some things can be useful. My mom seems to lose track of how many boyfriends she has. Or had. Either way, moms seems prone to carelessness. I just hoped that, in my absence, my mom wouldn't lose her head over this Andy lawyer person. But I couldn't worry about that for very long because it was barbecue night, and we were all looking forward to it.

CHAPTER 9

Mrs. Reeve was wearing— according to her—a comedy barbecue apron. And she looked pretty ridiculous in it. The figure of a muscle-bound male in swimming trunks with Mrs. Reeve's head sprouting out of the top wasn't so much comic as gross, particularly as her two grayish blond braids dangled either side of a hairy male chest.

"Grody!" Amber declared, stuffing shrimp in her mouth and washing them down with Coke as Mrs. Reeve shuffled off to the shed to get some more charcoal.

"Have you spoken to Mom, yet?" Zoe asked her, the ends of her curly blond hair still wet from her swim.

"Not yet," said Amber, rolling her eyes at me.

"Come ON, Amber, do it now!" Zoe yelled. "You can't keep putting it off, you have to tell her you've lost Silver."

"Get lost yourself, Zoe!" exclaimed Amber, helping herself to another shrimp. "Anyone would think you were the elder sister instead of me. Just leave me alone, will you?"

"Someone has to be responsible," mumbled Zoe.

"Just how valuable is your Silver horse?" asked Ellie. "My dad has a big bronze of a greyhound at home. It's really valuable, worth thousands of dollars and almost a hundred years old. Is Silver worth as much as that?"

"Probably," said Amber, gloomily, twirling her red hair around her fingers, piling it up high on the top of her head and pushing one of the barbecue skewers through it to keep it in place. A few tendrils fell and bounced around her neck—she looked really glamorous and about seventeen. I wished I could do that with my hair—only it's dark, reddish brown and really thick. If I tried to keep it on top of my head with a skewer, I'd have to hammer it into my skull. Which wouldn't be such a good look, I'm thinking.

"It's not just that," interrupted Zoe, "Amber's always losing things. I always told her she couldn't be trusted with something so valuable."

"You just love it, don't you?" Amber exploded. "You always wanted Silver and said you'd look after him better than me, so now you've got your wish. Happy?"

"What wish?"

"You told everyone I'd lose Silver, and now I have. You were right. You must be happy!"

"Er, my mom's got a new boyfriend—Andy," I said, hoping to distract the pair of them. "Apparently, Mom's very excited, says he might be The One, whatever that means."

"New dad material?" asked Bean, eyeing up the sausages on the barbecue. She was keeping out of the Amber and Zoe argument and I didn't blame her.

"Hope not!" I replied, "he hasn't a hair on his head, apparently. Totally bald!"

"Our dad's bald," said Amber. "As a coot!"

"What's a coot?" I asked.

"No idea!" laughed Amber. "But whatever it is, it must be bald."

"Hey, Grace, have you heard from your mom?" Bean asked.

Grace screwed up her face and nodded. "Yup," she said, "but she can't bully me over the phone, so I don't mind." Grace had lightened up considerably without her mom breathing down her neck, especially after jumping. She'd even picked out all of Shadow's hooves without any help. Yesterday, she'd been convinced he would kick her to pieces if she went anywhere near a hoof. Today, she was trainee farrier material.

"How about you, Ellie?" asked Amber, eager to keep the conversation away from her dreaded phone call home.

And that's when things went all weird. Ellie, who until now had been rather quiet, suddenly turned and fled toward the house like a swarm of bees was after her. Just like that. One minute she was there with us, chewing on a hunk of French bread like a dog with a bone, the next we were treated to a view of her back as she disappeared through the farmhouse door, wailing.

"What just happened?" asked Zoe.

"No quite sure," murmured Bean.

"Do you think we ought to go after her?" Amber asked.

"You can if you want," her sister replied.

"I don't know, she's so moody. One minute she's bragging about stuff we all know isn't true, the next she's sulking and quiet. She gives me the creeps," said Amber. "You go."

Mrs. Reeve returned, puffing, with a bag of charcoal.

Of course, she asked where Ellie was. So we told her. And then it was Mrs. Reeve's turn to go all weird.

"What did you do?" she asked earnestly, like we'd attacked Ellie with a bread roll or something.

"Nothing!" exclaimed Zoe. "One minute she was with us, the next she was gone."

"She's weird!" said Amber.

"What were you all talking about?" Mrs. Reeve asked, looking worried rather than angry.

"Not much," I said. "Grace's mom, I think."

Mrs. Reeve swallowed hard. "Amber, make sure nothing on the barbecue burns. I'll be right back," and, plastic novelty apron crackling, Mrs. R. jogged hurriedly toward the house, braids a-bobbing.

"Right," said Amber, wielding a barbecue fork and stuffing her chest out in mock importance, "I'm in charge!"

"Think again," I said, helping myself to a sausage and stuffing it into a roll.

"Perhaps she's ill," mused Grace.

"Who?" asked Bean.

"Ellie of course," cried Zoe. "You're like a goldfish, Bean. They have a memory which only lasts about three seconds."

"How do you know?" Bean asked with perfect logic. "I mean, you can't know how long a goldfish's memory lasts, can you?"

"Know what?" asked Amber, grinning at me.

"Oh, very funny!" said Zoe.

"Perhaps Ellie's not ill. Perhaps she's crazy. Perhaps

she's gone absolutely insane!" suggested Amber, darkly. "Mrs. Reeve will have to call the men in white coats to take her away in a straitjacket, and High Grove Farm will be closed down and we'll all be on the news. Wouldn't that be cool?"

"What's a straitjacket?" asked Grace.

"It locks your arms together so you can't do any harm to yourself or anyone else," I explained.

"How do you know that, Pia?" Amber said, her eyes glinting. Two more tendrils of hair escaped the skewer and drifted around her face. "Have you been restrained by one? Do you have a dark history you'd hate us to know about?"

"She murders people who get on her nerves," said Bean. "So I'd shut up if I were you."

"Shhh, they're coming back," said Grace and we all turned to see Ellie and Mrs. Reeve coming toward us. That Ellie had been crying was obvious. Her eyes were red and puffy and she sniffed a lot.

"OK girls, let's get dig in to this barbecue," said Mrs. Reeves, a bit over-brightly. "Oh," she continued, as she spotted the almost empty rack over the glowing charcoal, "I see you've helped yourselves."

"We were starving!" said Bean. "But we've saved you some, Ellie. Here, have a burger."

There were no explanations and it was clear that questions were not to be asked so nothing more was said. I really couldn't take to Ellie; she'd done nothing to endear herself to anyone on this vacation. She was either going on about getting a show jumping pony and bragging about her riding at home or she was all quiet and sulky. I couldn't figure her out at all.

After eating a burger, some salad and a decent amount of chocolate chip ice cream, Ellie was back to her usual, irritating self. Almost. The mood had lightened considerably due to one of Mrs. R.'s braids dangling into the barbecue and catching fire. Quick-thinking Amber had doused the flames by emptying her can of Coke over them. The sight of Mrs. Reeve with her one blond braid and one, singed and dripping gave us all the giggles.

I was beginning to feel a bit strange, having spent every waking hour of the last two days with the same half-a-dozen or so people, so I took myself off to sit on a swing someone had fashioned out of a plank and two ropes hanging from a tree, and flipped open my cell phone. I was missing Drummer and was suddenly desperate to hear from Katy.

I had two messages: one from Dad, saying he hoped I was having a great time and that he and Lyn would like us all to get together when I was home again (boohoo!). The other was from James. Woo-hoo!

Hey, PW, it read, hurry up and come home. My heart started racing—he was missing me! I can't talk to Moth without you-know-who!

My heart settled down to its usual pace. You-know-who was our code name for Epona. James was missing my statuette, not me. Or maybe, I thought, pathetically clutching at straws, that was just an excuse. I know, I know, desperate, or what?

Annoyed at allowing myself to be so pathetic, I dialed Katy's number, hoping for some good news that wouldn't juggle around with my heart. She'd be at the yard now, checking on Bluey and Drum and turning them out for the night. I wanted to know what Drum had been up to and how Katy had done at the first of her two Easter hunter trials. It rang forever and then, finally...

"Huddo," said a voice. It was Katy's voice, sort of— if Katy was wearing a clown's nose and happened to be speaking from the inside of a bag with air as thick as pudding.

"What's wrong with you?" I asked, bewildered.

"I'm thick," said Katy in her new voice.

"Don't be an idiot, you're really smart," I said.

"No, thick. ILL," Katy explained, sniffing.

"Oh, poor you. What have you got?" I asked her.

"Fur-loo. Horwid, stoopid, inconveedient fur-loo!" she replied, obviously not impressed.

"You sound like you've got a speech impediment," I told her.

"That's helbfoll. Makes me feel buch bedder," she sniffed. "Dow go away, I'm dyin'."

"How's Drummer?" I said, wondering who was looking after him. It sounded like Katy was out of action. Maybe Dee was seeing to him—she was caring for Tiffany for Bean. I could just imagine how annoyed she would be, having two extra ponies to feed and check over. Or—and my heart did another flip at the thought—maybe James was caring for Drum. I wouldn't mind that.

"Oh, Peer, don't be bad ad me," Katy said, swallowing hard.

"What? Oh, you mean mad. Of course I won't be mad. You have got someone to look after Drum, haven't you?" My heart started thudding in my chest. What if Drum had been left to fend for himself? A vision of my bay pony looking forlornly over his half-door wafted before my eyes. An image of the other ponies being mucked out and fed, of Drummer being ignored. Of Drum gazing down the drive waiting for me to come and feed him. Waiting in vain. Was anyone caring for my Drummer?

"She off-ed, and you dow she takes really good care of Bambi," Katy continued.

I held my breath. NOOOOOOOO, I thought, my head spinning. Anyone but her. Katy had to be kidding!

"Are you telling me…?" I began shakily, already know-ing the answer and not quite knowing how I felt about it.

"Cat will see to Drum's every need, you dow she will. I'm sorry Peer, I didn't dow what else to do. Please don't be bad ad me. She's lookin' arvta Bluey, too."

I felt numb all over. My darling pony was being cared for by my arch enemy, Catriona.

Oh pooh, pooh, pooh!

CHAPTER 10

WHEN I WOKE ON Wednesday morning, I felt more tired than I had the night before. I'd tossed and turned all night thinking about Catriona caring for Drummer. Why did it have to be her? Why couldn't it have been anyone, anyone else? Dee-Dee, James, Leanne—even ancient Mrs. Bradley with Henry would be an improvement on Cat. Katy had obviously been desperate. It wasn't until I'd eaten breakfast that I realized Katy must be missing her hunter trials. How selfish was I, worrying about Drum when poor Katy was ill in bed and missing the competitions she and Bluey had been so looking forward to? I hadn't even asked her about them, I'd been so distracted by the thought of Cat looking after Drummer.

I'd have to be grateful to Cat, I thought. I'd have to thank her! Drum would probably enjoy being taken out to the field and brought in again with Cat's skewbald mare. Drum felt the same way about Bambi as I did about James.

But why did it have to be Cat? And why did she volunteer? I kept thinking. And thinking. And I couldn't even call her and find out about Drummer, which was just the worst thing. No, the worst thing was imagining my beloved pony being cared for by Cat. What if he liked her? What if she poisoned his mind about me? What if they got on so well together, he didn't want me to come back home? I couldn't get it out of my mind, not even with the exciting promise of today's mystery activity. It went around and around in my head, driving me nuts.

And there wasn't a thing I could do about it. I was miles away from home and unable to do anything but think and worry and worry some more.

The Wednesday mystery activity had been given a big build-up. Lots of winks and dramatic eye-widening by Annabelle and Sharon whenever it had been mentioned or asked about, so big things were expected by everyone. I hoped it was good—it needed to be to take my mind off the disturbing news about Cat. But the mystery event wasn't scheduled until after lunch. This morning, we had the daily lesson.

Sprout was almost friendly when I got him in from the field.

"Hello," he said gruffly as I offered him an apple I'd snitched from breakfast.

"Thanks," he said, munching thoughtfully. "Golden Delicious," he mumbled, dribbling apple foam over his chest and on to my arms.

"Yes," I agreed, trying to brush the sticky stuff off and only spreading it about instead.

"I prefer Granny Smiths," he said.

"Sorry, that's all they had," I told him, putting on his harness and leading him in to his stable and trying, unsuccessfully, to stop thinking about Catriona doing the same thing with my pony at home. Bean had gone all wide-eyed at me when I told her who Katy had got to care for Drummer.

"How do you feel about that?" she'd asked me.

"How do you think?" I'd replied, dramatically. "But it's not like I can do anything about it, not from here. But then…"

"What?"

"Well, do you think James would look after Drum for me, if I asked him?"

Bean had pulled a face. "Yeah, I guess he would, but how do you think Cat would feel, being usurped?" she'd said.

"But you know she hates me," I'd replied. "She can't want to look after Drummer. She'd probably be relieved to get rid of the responsibility."

"Didn't Katy say she'd offered? She might think you're making a statement about her ability to care for your pony, she could be extending the olive branch to you— you know, being friendly," Bean had pointed out. "And besides," she'd continued, "Cat's OK—you two just hit it off all wrong to start with and now neither of you can forget it."

"She almost got Drummer stolen, have you forgotten that?" I'd cried, remembering how Cat had struck a deal with one of the travelers. "What if she gets someone else to steal him while I'm away?"

"You're over-reacting," Bean had said soothingly. Only she hadn't said it quite convincingly enough.

Oh pooh again, I'd thought. I'm stuck with it. Drummer's stuck with it. How would I feel if Cat said she didn't want me to look after Bambi, especially if I'd offered, put myself out, even? I knew I would feel offended. Like I wasn't good enough, even though I'd look after Bambi like she was my own. Things were bad enough between Cat and me. If I replaced her with someone else, things could only get worse. I didn't really think she'd be horrible to Drum. What really worried me, and I hated to admit it, was the thought of Cat getting close to Drum, of sharing with him special moments like I shared with him. I was in agony imagining it.

"Pooh!" I'd said with feeling.

"That's mature!" Bean had remarked.

Despite having other things on my mind, the morning lesson was fantastic. I managed to get my act together in the first half when we did flatwork, and got Sprout to go at exactly the pace I wanted all the time, by using my half-halts and by concentrating really hard on correcting any changes of pace he put in—both faster and slower. Annabelle was gushing with her praise and I got two 'very goods' and a 'well done, Pia'!

Sharon put up a course of jumps for the second half of the lesson, telling us that a gymkhana was planned for Friday and it would include a jumping class. (Annabelle didn't do much to help, just pointed to where she wanted the jumps to be while Sharon huffed and puffed and dragged wings and poles about). The course was nothing

87

big, but it was still tricky. First to go was Amber who, determined not to let Sorrel dump her, rode very strongly, proving that she was a good rider when she could be bothered. Sorrel approached each jump in a zigzag way, grumbling about having to jump, but Amber kept her rein contact and legged on so the chestnut mare had nowhere to go but over. Everyone cheered (even Zoe) as she flew over the last jump and Amber let out a whoop of delight. Sorrel said nothing, which made a change.

Sprout and I almost managed a clear round—but a run-out at the second-from-last jump gave us three faults. I was to blame as I'd let Sprout run on instead of keeping him between my leg and hand. I had to remember that! The faster we went, the easier it was to for Sprout to go around the jump, not over it, Annabelle reminded me.

Cherokee's complaint-of-the-day concerned his back. He kept saying he had twinges and that he shouldn't be jumping, but because no one could hear him but me, he wasn't excused from anything and Bean made a good job of getting him round the small course without any mishaps. Used to Tiffany's eccentric way of jumping, Cherokee was a piece of cake by comparison!

Ellie was still looking messy on Harry but he carried her round without her having to do much work, gaining eight faults. Harry made a couple of comments about being all heart, and I had to agree with him. He could have run out at each jump, Ellie's reins were so long, but he gallantly jumped each one, just rolling a couple of poles. Grace, on the other hand, her confidence in her pony sky-high, had morphed into a budding show jumper on Shadow—she tackled the whole course with a huge grin and Shadow rose to the occasion. When the gray took a hard look at the last jump, Grace determinedly used her legs and urged him over, earning another loud cheer from everyone watching. And under Zoe's guidance, even the inexperienced Dot-2-Dot managed a clear round.

"You've all been wonderful!" gushed Annabelle, as we lined up and patted our ponies. "You're really getting to grips with your mounts and improving in leaps and bounds."

As we walked the ponies in, I noticed Bean's hands were bare.

"Forgotten your beloved new gloves?" I asked her, patting Sprout's neck.

Bean looked worried. "I can't find them," she replied. "I put them on the bench in the yard, together with my hat, when I came back from riding yesterday, but when I went back for them, I could only find my hat."

"Are you positive you had them?" I asked her. "You know what you're like."

"Yes, I know, but I remember because Ellie was being useless with Harry and she practically backed him into Cherokee as I was putting my hat on the bench. I distinctly remember stuffing my gloves into my hat as I put it down."

"So how could your gloves disappear if they were in your hat?"

"Exactly!"

"Have you asked Sharon? She checks around the yard at night."

"Yes, I asked Sharon and Annabelle, and neither had seen them. It's like they just disappeared and I *know* they were there."

"Perhaps someone else picked them up," I said without thinking.

"Yes," said Bean, "that's the conclusion I reached."

We looked at each other.

"You mean…" I said.

Bean frowned. "I just know they were definitely there."

"You do sometimes, er, forget things," I said as tactfully as I could. Bean was off in her own world a lot of the time, so she could have been mistaken.

"I'll have another look," Bean said quickly. "But if I can't find them, I'm going to ask everyone else whether they know anything."

"Mmmm, OK," I replied, a sinking feeling nagging at my stomach. I felt worried for Epona without really knowing why and I curled my fingers around the tiny stone statue, safe in my pocket. What if Epona went missing, too? It didn't bear thinking about.

We turned the ponies out for the afternoon and watched as they wandered off to graze, chatting to one another. Dot rolled and rolled and rolled. Harry and Sprout stood next to one another, chewing each other's withers in a mutual groom and Shadow ground to a halt just inside the gateway and did his favorite thing—sleep. Sorrel and Cherokee swapped grumbles under a tree. Sorrel was still indignant at having been made to jump and Cherokee insisted she was lucky she didn't have a bad back, like he had.

Of course, we had to clean tack before lunch but everyone did it in record time—we were all looking forward to the mystery activity.

"What do you think it will be?" asked Zoe, wiping Dot's stirrups dry.

"A rodeo!" exclaimed Amber. "Or maybe trying vaulting, or visiting a racehorse stable!"

"Wow, you've got a vivid imagination!" said Grace. "I can't think of a single thing it might be."

"Perhaps we're going to a horse rescue stable," suggested Bean. "The one Cherokee came from. Annabelle told me he only went there because his owner couldn't afford to keep him anymore. He hadn't been mistreated, or anything."

"Or an Olympic training yard—or someone famous!" Zoe said, rubbing saddle soap like crazy into Dot's browband.

"Got any suggestions, Ellie?" said Amber, looking over to her. "You've been very quiet since we got back."

Ellie just shrugged her shoulders without saying anything. We were getting used to Ellie. If she wasn't quiet, she was bragging about something or other. We were all getting a bit fed up with the bragging, so we tended to switch off whenever she started up, which probably prompted her silence.

"I bet it won't be anything as spectacular as visiting anyone famous," I said, putting Sprout's bridle back together. "It might be a tour of a feed mill or a saddle maker, or something like that."

"Nah!" said Amber as she threw her dirty water down the drain. "I bet it's much more exciting after Annabelle's big build-up. Like trying western riding—or side-saddle. That would be soooo cool, I've always wanted to try sitting sideways."

"Well, why don't you?" asked her sister. "Just sit sideways on Sorrel. I'd love to see how that works out."

Amber laughed. "I might!" she cried. "Anyone wanna try it with me?"

"No," Grace replied. "I have enough trouble riding astride. I hope it *isn't* side-saddle."

I thought of Epona, sitting sideways on her horse. Copying her would be cool.

"Has anyone seen my new riding gloves?" asked Bean. I held my breath.

"No," said Ellie.

"Sorry, no," replied Grace.

"Can't say I have," added Zoe.

"What do they look like?" asked Amber.

"Leather, brown, soft, supple, gorgeous," said Bean with a slight edge to her voice. "Expensive," she added.

"Where did you lose them?" Zoe asked.

"I didn't say I'd lost them," said Bean.

"Oh, I thought you said you couldn't find them," said

Amber, concentrating on putting all the straps on Sorrel's bridle into their runners and keepers so that they didn't flap around.

"I'm saying that yesterday they were on the bench in the yard, and today they're not. So I wondered whether anyone had seen them," explained Bean.

Everyone shook their heads. No one seemed to pick up on Bean's implication that the gloves had been taken, not lost. As my heart thumped I looked from face to face, wondering whether anyone knew more than they were letting on, but no one looked guilty. It was horrible to think that we suspected one of our fellow vacationers of theft, but Bean was certain that she'd left her gloves with her hat.

"If I go to hell when I die," mused Amber, as Annabelle approached with her clipboard, "it will be full of Annabelles all making me clean tack. And the funny thing is, if Zoe goes to heaven, she'll be met with exactly the same thing!"

"Lunch is ready, girls," announced Annabelle, "and we don't want to be late for our exciting mystery activity, do we?"

"What is it?" asked Amber, for the zillionth time.

Annabelle just crinkled up her eyes and shook her head. It was very annoying. She did brandish her clipboard around, however, writing things down as she tweaked and inspected our tack.

"This," Bean grumbled under her breath, "is not fun. It is not as billed in the *Pony* mag comp. Win a riding vacation, it said. A va-*ca*-tion! This is boot camp!"

Bean just hated cleaning tack.

Lunch was punctuated at regular intervals by Amber asking Annabelle to reveal the mystery activity.

"Is it side-saddle riding?" she asked.

"Nope," replied Annabelle, shaking her head—again.

"Is it…" said Amber, listing every possibility that had been suggested earlier. Annabelle denied them all, her smugness growing by degrees at every suggestion.

"Stop asking," I hissed in Amber's direction, "you're just making Annabelle's day by going on about it. Play it cool!"

"I'm just seeing how smug she can get," Amber whispered back, winking at me. "I'm hoping she'll get a smug overload and lose her marbles!"

Eventually it was time for us all to buckle up in the High Grove Farm van with Annabelle at the wheel. She had changed into a disturbingly low-cut top and some extra tight designer jeans, as well as adding some cheek bones via some blush, and some plumping lip gloss. When Amber saw her, she raised her eyes at me in surprise. Sharon, needless to say, was staying at home to do yard duties.

Our excitement increased with every mile and eventually, Annabelle pulled into a driveway lined with trees. Someone had draped a sheet over the sign by the road so we still didn't know where we were. It was all very cloak-and-dagger. Zoe grumbled that anyone would think we were going to see somebody famous. Amber immediately latched on to this idea and ran with it.

"Everybody act cool when we get out, just be really calm about it when Annabelle tells us who it is," she added. "She'll be soo disappointed when we don't freak out."

"That will be totally awesome!" I said to Bean.

She nodded in agreement. "Can you imagine what the others back home will say if we meet someone famous?" she said, grinning. "Cat will be livid! I'm going to make sure I get an autograph."

My heart string twanged. Was Cat with my beloved Drummer right now? Was she getting closer and closer to him with every moment? Was I fading from Drummer's memory, gradually being replaced by Cat? I shook my head, trying to shake the image from my mind.

Annabelle parked in a gravel parking lot and we all piled out.

"Remember," Amber hissed to everyone, "play it cool."

We all followed Annabelle to a spotless yard where several horses, including a cob with a Roman nose, looked at us curiously over their half-doors. And then we heard footsteps.

"They're coming!" whispered Amber, turning to get the first glimpse as the footsteps behind the stables got nearer and louder.

"Hello everyone," said a man with graying hair. Then, as his twinkling eyes saw me his face split into a grin.

"Hello, Pia," he said.

CHAPTER 11

FOURTEEN PAIRS OF EYES swung around toward me and several mouths dropped in astonishment. Annabelle blinked several times as Alex Willard, possibly the most famous horse behaviorist in the world, walked across and gave me a hug. I couldn't believe he remembered me. It was astonishing—and totally thrilling!

"Pia and I met when we were on the TV together," he explained to everyone. Like it was a perfectly ordinary thing to do—meet on TV. My heart sank.

"On TV? Together?" asked Annabelle incredulously, looking at me anew.

"That's right, on the *Cecily Armstrong* show," explained Alex.

"You? And Pia?" said Annabelle, confused. Her gaze alternated between me and her hero and everyone else except Bean looked at me in amazement, too. I felt myself go hot and realized that my face was turning crimson.

"But you know about Pia, don't you?" Alex continued, unaware of the damage he was doing.

Oh no, I thought, please don't tell them…

"What do you mean?" said Amber gleefully, her eyes like saucers. "What is there to know?"

"You know she's the Pony Whisperer? She can talk to ponies—and horses, of course. I watched *Pony Whispering Live!* Pia. You were amazing—that poor pony who had been a war horse. Do you know what happened to her?"

"Um, I think her owner was going to move her to a yard where she couldn't hear the gun shots." I mumbled. Shoving my hands in my pockets it seemed that Epona leapt into my hand, mocking me. I bet if I could hear my stone statue talking instead of ponies I'd have heard *ha, ha, ha!* I hated to think of how the others were going to take the news of my pony-whispering powers.

"I said I knew you!" exclaimed Amber, pointing at me. "I saw *Pony Whispering Live!* It's you, Pia Edwards, the Pony Whisperer! You wait till I tell everyone at the riding school. They'll never believe I've met you. They'll be soooo jealous!"

"Wow!" breathed Grace. "Can you really hear what ponies are saying?"

I knew what was coming...

"So can you hear what our ponies are saying?" asked Zoe, the truth dawning on her at last.

"What's Sorrel like?" yelled Amber, jumping up and down. "Does she like me? Is she really cool? What's her favorite thing to do?"

"How about Shadow?" asked Grace. "Can you tell him how much I love him?"

"You can tell him yourself, he can understand you, Grace," I said.

"And Dot?" asked Zoe. "Oh, I know she's sensitive and intelligent, I don't need you to tell me that!"

You see, this is why I hate anyone knowing about my PW status. How could I disillusion poor Zoe? How could I tell Amber that Sorrel was grumpy and totally superior? I was going to have to be a bit economical with the truth if I didn't want to ruin anyone's vacation. Especially mine.

"I bet you knew!" cried Amber, poking Bean in the side.

"Ouch!" said Bean. "I'm as surprised as you are," she lied, shooting me a glance.

"Can you hear absolutely everything ponies say?" demanded Ellie.

Amber softly punched my arm. "How come you didn't say anything before now?"

Annabelle's face distorted into an I'm-not-sure-about-hearing-ponies sort of look, before creasing back into her familiar, plastered-on smile. "We'll talk about that later. Now, we're here to see how Alex Willard trains and helps horses, remember?"

Alex smiled in her direction and I heard a small sigh escape from Annabelle.

"It looks like our Annabelle's got the hots for Alex Willard!" I whispered to Bean.

"You don't need to be a pony whisperer to figure that one out," Bean whispered back. "She might as well run a flag up a pole, play a fanfare on the trumpet and wear a T-shirt with *I Love Alex Willard* on the front."

As I tried to rub that image out of my mind Alex showed us round his stable yard. It was gorgeous. Around three sides, old barns and brick buildings had been converted into stables. There were hanging baskets full of lavender and white flowers, lovely wooden benches in the yard, commandeered by dozing cats, and every black-and-white door framed an equine head. Two old painted wagon wheels were propped up against the walls and everywhere was spick-and-span.

Then I heard the voices.

"Oh no, oh no, oh no, oh no, oh no..." said a bay thoroughbred as we walked round the yard.

"Stop panicking," a strawberry roan cob with a Roman nose in the next door stable told him. "No one's coming to ride you. They're just visiting, they come every week."

"Are they here for the fight?" said a stunning gray with a long, flowing lead-gray mane.

"I keep telling you, we don't hold fights here," the cob told him.

"These horses are some of the cases I'm working with at the moment," explained Alex, walking up to the strawberry roan cob. The gelding looked at us trustingly. It didn't seem the sort of horse that needed Alex's help. Specializing in training horses with problems, Alex was famous for helping horses and ponies that had issues. As one of the world's most respected trainers and behaviorists, he mimicked the horse's own behavior and communication to get to the bottom of their problems—most of them caused by humans. I was a regular visitor to his website and he was my total hero.

"What's wrong with this one?" asked Ellie.

"What's his name?" whispered Grace, reaching out to stroke the roan's nose.

"His name is Clutter," said Alex, smiling at Grace, "and his owners say he's the most disobedient horse in the world."

"But he looks like such a sweetheart!" said Zoe.

"He has no confidence and hates being in the lead," Alex said.

Clutter leaned over and had a chat with all of us, loving the fuss. "I don't suppose any of you have brought treats with you?" he said. "Sugar lumps? The odd carrot? It's kinda rude, visiting without gifts, wouldn't you say?"

"We were told they weren't allowed," I said without thinking.

Everyone turned and looked at me. Well, I thought, the game's up now so what do I have to lose?

"What are you saying there, Pony Whisperer?" said Alex, smiling. "What's Clutter telling you?"

"He's only interested in whether we've brought him any treats," I replied.

"While you're here, could you ask him to stop being so resistant to his riders?" laughed Alex.

"Oh, Alex, you are sweet," sighed Annabelle, "to go along with Pia's um, ideas."

"Didn't you see *Pony Whispering Live!*?" Amber asked her. "Pia talked to two horses and helped them."

"Yes, I saw it, too," said Zoe. "Awesome!"

"I wish I'd seen it," said Grace.

"I'm sure you can't talk to horses," muttered Ellie, almost to herself. She sounded like Cat, who's a bit of a broken record as far as my pony-whispering title goes.

"Well that's all you know!" Amber leapt to my defense, rounding on Ellie. "Why are you so down on everything all the time? You're such a grouch."

Annabelle put her arm around Ellie. "That's no way to talk to Ellie, Amber," she said. "Apologize!"

"For what?" asked Amber. "No way am I apologizing, she is a grouch. And when she's not being a grouch, she's sulking on her own somewhere!"

"You know, all these negative vibes are very bad for the horses," Alex said in his usual, laid-back manner.

"Oh, sorry," said Amber, looking mortified. "I don't mind apologizing to you," she added, grinning at Alex. Alex grinned back.

Zoe whispered, "You're such a suck-up!" to her sister, but Amber ignored her. She had fallen under Alex's spell and wasn't going to let Zoe spoil her day.

"So Clutter here is undergoing some riding therapy," the great man continued, patting the roan. "Clutter is a horse who finds it difficult to go anywhere without a strong personality to take the lead. Even though I'm on top of him, rather than in front of him, I'm working on making him realize that when he's with me—or any other rider— he's not alone. The rider will make the decisions and all he has to do is follow their lead. If he thinks it's all up to him, it blows his mind a bit."

"How long will it take to cure him?" asked Zoe, stroking Clutter's pink nose.

The cob licked the palm of her hand. "I'll just have to make do with the salt from your palm," he slurped, between licks.

"Impossible to say," said Alex, shaking his head. "Some horses respond in a matter of moments, others take much longer. The deciding factor is how his owners ride him, they need to have the confidence to be Clutter's leader."

"How come Clutter's like he is?" asked Grace.

"Oh, usually it's because a rider doesn't notice when a horse they are riding hesitates," said Alex. "If they don't give the horse confidence there and then, the problem can grow until the horse refuses to leave the yard. With the brave horses, that doesn't happen. Others, like Clutter here, can lose all confidence."

"Who's this, and can I have him?" asked Zoe, making friends with the gray. He was a totally stunning horse with the longest, crinkliest mane and forelock ever. They tumbled from his crest like a rippling, silver waterfall, splashing and foaming around his face and neck.

"That's Verano. He's Spanish and I'm still trying to discover the secrets locked in his soul," Alex replied.

We moved along to Verano's stable.

"He doesn't seem to have any hang-ups," said Bean as Verano nuzzled her hand.

"He's a wonderful, giving horse," Alex told her. "Amazing to ride. I believe he was intended for work in the bullring but was sold when his owners decided he wasn't brave enough."

"Bullfighting is so cruel," said Amber with feeling.

"People have argued about it for years," said Alex.

"Surely you're against Spanish bullfighting?" asked Bean. "They kill the bull!"

"Yes," agreed Alex, nodding, "but the bulls have a good life in the Andalusian hills before they are big and strong enough to fight. It's true that their last moments are filled with cruelty and pain, but the Spanish believe that a death in the bullring is filled with glory, better than the death a steer faces in the slaughter house. They greatly admire the bull."

Everyone went quiet, comparing the two bovine lives. I felt a bit sick.

"I think I'll become vegetarian," said Grace. "Then cows won't be slaughtered for me."

"But what about your leather jodhpur boots?" said Amber.

"And saddles and bridles are made of leather, aren't they?" said Bean, frowning.

"I'm going to get synthetic tack for my pony," said Ellie.

"So what exactly is Verano's problem, Alex?" Annabelle asked brightly, hoping to change the subject and lighten the mood.

"General jumpiness. The grooms tell me he has a real thing about wheelbarrows, snorts at them and refuses to let them go behind him. We have to make sure he's in his stable whenever a wheelbarrow goes past. If he's tied up outside, he acts as if they're dragons."

"Why on earth are you scared of wheelbarrows?" I whispered almost to myself, absentmindedly.

"I have to face the wheel," the horse replied, matter-of-factly. I was surprised he answered my question. And his answer prompted another one.

"Why do you have to face the wheel?" I whispered.

Alex looked intently from me to Verano. "What is he saying, Pia?" he asked urgently.

Everyone turned from Verano to me.

"Because I have to. Because I have been trained to. Because to turn my back on the wheel is unacceptable," the horse whispered. He didn't seem to think it strange that I could hear him or that I was asking him questions.

"Why mustn't you turn your back on the wheel?" I asked. I couldn't understand why it was so important.

"The wheel is the bull. I must always face the bull—I must do exactly as my master bids me with his legs and his seat. I dance with the bull. I lure him in and dance around him. I cannot turn from him, cannot run from him. It is difficult, it is hard work, it is—how you say—stressful. I find it exhausting—mentally. My friend, Bruja, loved the work, but it is too much for me. When I see the wheel I see again the horns. It makes me fearful, remembering."

I repeated what Verano told me to Alex—and everyone else. Amber looked at me wide-eyed and excited, as did Zoe and Grace, but Ellie and Annabelle's faces showed doubt. Bean was used to me and looked just Bean-like, as usual, but Alex looked at me with total concentration and I could tell that his mind was working hard to make sense of what his troubled client was telling me.

"So the wheelbarrow is the bull, have I got that right?" Alex asked me.

I nodded. "That's what Verano is saying. But it doesn't make sense, does it?"

"Of course!" Alex looked like Bean when she finally understands what we've been saying to her. "That's how they train bullfighting horses!"

"To do what? Muck out?" giggled Amber.

"They don't use a real bull to train them," Alex explained. "They start with a person pushing a wheel around—it's like half a bicycle with horns on the handle-bars and looks a bit like a wheelbarrow. It sounds crazy, but it works—the person working the wheel can change direction instantly, just like a bull. That's why Verano acts so strangely when the wheelbarrows are on the yard! We'll have to re-train him—but wait, can you explain to him, Pia, can you explain that wheelbarrows are nothing to do with bull fighting, and that he will never again be asked to train for anything like that? His new life will never involve such vigorous work. He has nothing to fear now. He is never going back to his bullfighting days. Can you tell him that?"

"He can hear you," I said as the gray sighed and relaxed.

"Is this true?" he asked me.

I nodded. "Never," I said. "You will never work with the bull again, Verano. Your new life here will be completely bull-free."

Alex grinned. "I ought to employ you on a consultancy basis," he said, walking on and stopping outside the bay's stable. "What can you tell me about this horse, Pia?" Alex asked.

I looked at the beautiful thoroughbred head looking out over the door. A thin stripe of white ran all the way from between his eyes to his nose. His ears flicked back and forth and his nostrils opened and closed like mini bellows as he weaved from side-to-side over the half-door. That the horse was disturbed by all of us taking over the yard was fairly obvious—no pony-whispering powers were needed to deduce that.

"Please don't choose me, please not me, not me, not me, not me…" the thoroughbred muttered to himself, and the ear flicking and weaving got more agitated the closer I got.

"Why don't you want to be chosen?" I asked, patting his silky neck. "What are you scared of?"

The thoroughbred's eyes opened even wider. "Oh, oh, oh, can you hear me? Can you hear me? How come, how come?"

"Don't worry," I said softly. "I'm not going to choose you, just tell me what you're so scared of." I could feel everyone holding their breath behind me. It was so weird, doing this to order—something I hadn't done since I'd been asked to go on TV to do *Pony Whispering Live!*

"You're not going to ride me? You're not? You're not?" repeated the Thoroughbred, almost forgetting to weave in his relief.

"No. I just wonder why you don't want me to," I probed gently. Would the horse tell me why he was so fearful of being ridden? Had he been hurt?

"I don't like it, I don't, I don't. I don't know what they want. They keep changing their minds. I do everything I've been told to do, but they're never satisfied. I don't know what to do, I don't know what they want. Why do they keep changing their minds? Why? How am I supposed to know? How? How?"

I turned to Alex and repeated the thoroughbred's fears.

Alex nodded. "Lava Flow here used to be a racehorse. His new owner wants to show him in hack classes. The trouble is," Alex went on, aware that we were all listening intently and hanging on his every word, "racehorses are trained in a totally different way to most horses."

"How come?" asked Zoe. "How different?"

"Well, for a start, they're almost never asked to do anything by themselves—they are always exercised in a string, they always have other horses around them. And did you know that when you take up rein contact on a cantering racehorse, that's his cue to go faster?"

"No way!" exclaimed Amber.

"Oh yes," said Alex, nodding solemnly, his graying hair flopping over his face so he had to brush it back with one hand. "The more you pull, the faster a racehorse goes.

There are lots of other differences, too. Our job with Lava Flow is to retrain him. His new owner rode him exactly as she has ridden every other horse she's owned. Her problem was that the other horses weren't racehorses. It's not only poor Lava Flow who is confused, his owner is, too. My job is to re-train the horse and his rider together."

"So you train riders, too?" asked Amber. I wondered whether she was going to ask Alex for a lesson.

"Only with their horses," Alex replied. "You're completely right, Pia. We knew this horse's problem stemmed from his past training being incompatible with his new owner. But it isn't just the horse which has to adapt—his owner needs to understand and change her riding, too. I'm just glad he doesn't have any other problems we don't know about. The confusion will be easy to clear up and then Lava Flow should be a lot more relaxed and happy with himself and his environment."

"The horses here are so lucky—coming to you, Alex," said Annabelle, even more in love with her hero than before. Behind her, Amber rolled her eyes and pretended to gag.

"How come you know so much about horses?" asked Bean. "Oh," she said, her hand flying to her mouth, "I didn't mean that to sound the way it did. I mean, how did you learn it all?"

"By watching horses, by thinking about them, by trying to think like them," Alex explained with a smile. "The more you watch horses and try to understand what motivates them, you learn all the time. No time spent watching horses is wasted. If you can take time to just sit and watch a group of horses or ponies in a field, you can learn so much."

"Remember to sit safely *outside* the field, won't you?" interjected Annabelle, her health-and-safety hat firmly nailed to her head.

"Oh, absolutely, Annabelle," Alex agreed. Annabelle visibly melted. Honestly, Alex must have noticed, or perhaps he was used to women falling at his feet. Even my mom had flirted with him when she met him at the TV studios. I shuddered when I remembered. So not a good memory!

"Any more questions?" Alex asked us.

"Have you ever met a horse you couldn't help?" Amber asked.

"There have been a few I haven't been able to fathom," Alex admitted. "Some horses have been so abused— usually unintentionally—that they're on the verge of madness. It's always sad when that occurs, but I'm not a magician, I can only do so much. Sometimes I ask Emma Ellison—you'll remember her, Pia—to assist me. She can sometimes reach horses that have shut off from humans too much for me to connect with. But of course, if I ever get another horse I can't help in future, I know the Pony Whisperer is there to give me a hand!" and he winked at me and I felt myself go red. Was he teasing or did he mean it?

I did remember Emma Ellison—self-confessed horse

healer. She had been a kind of full of herself but Alex thought a lot of her so I reckoned Emma had to have something.

"Do you think nervous riders can become good riders?" Grace whispered.

"I think nervous riders often make the best riders," Alex said, smiling. "They are often more empathic and intuitive, and their sensitivity makes horses like and trust them. So the answer is definitely yes—if a nervous person works at their riding, it will pay off."

"What does empathic mean?" asked Bean.

"Oh, sorry—it means someone who can put themselves in another person's place and sympathize with their feelings. That's empathy. To be a good horse trainer, you need to be able to put yourself in each horse's skin and see things as they see them. It's easy to judge from our own perspective, but we don't always know how horses view things, and what has happened to make them the way they are. Now let me take you all for a tour of my place. And feel free to ask any questions as we go around."

We had the most fantastic tour. As well as the stables we saw the indoor and outdoor schools, a training pen, the most gorgeous tack room (which would have passed any inspection Annabelle and her clipboard cared to make), an immaculate feed room and Alex's office. There were photographs of Alex with famous horsey people, and press cuttings and features of him all over the walls.

"Is this you with Zara Phillips?" Amber asked, pointing to a picture taken at Badminton Horse Trials in England.

Alex nodded.

"What's she like?" said Amber.

"Honestly Amber, what are you like?" said Zoe, digging her in the ribs.

"What?" said Amber.

Alex laughed and told us about the famous people he'd met during the course of his career and answered all our questions, although he must have answered the same ones time and time again. And then it was time to go. We all said good-bye, patted the horses again (they said good-bye too, although no one heard them but me), and then climbed back into the van.

"That was just awesome!" Amber declared.

"Totally fantastic!" her sister agreed.

"Wow, you two agreeing with each other—that has to be a first!" observed Bean.

"I wish Alex Willard was my dad," muttered Grace.

"Oh wow, so do I!" yelled Bean. "Although I do love my own dad, of course," she mumbled, hastily.

"I'm going to be a horse behaviorist when I leave school," said Ellie.

"The man's amazing," I said, looking out of the van window and watching the stables get smaller and smaller as Annabelle drove us away and back toward High Grove Farm.

I know, I thought as we turned a corner and Alex's yard disappeared altogether, my mind returning to my big problem, I'll ask James to keep an eye on Drum for me. Without Cat knowing. That wouldn't be too much to ask, would it? He'd understand.

I pulled my cell out of my pocket and started texting. Then I read it back. It made me sound desperate, and jealous and insecure. Snapping my phone shut I shoved it back in my pocket, the text unsent. It made me sound all those things because they were true. And I didn't want anyone else to know that. Except me.

CHAPTER 12

SELF-ELECTED SOCIAL SECRETARY AMBER had decided that Wednesday night was Midnight Feast Night.

"We absolutely have to have one," she declared, tearing off her T-shirt, which had been well and truly slimed by Verano's slobber and replacing it with a clean one with the slogan *I'm such a horsey babe* across the front. "It's compulsory on a riding vacation, everyone knows that. And besides," she added, flashing me a look, "I want to tell everyone at the riding school that I've midnight-feasted with the Pony Whisperer!"

I felt my toes curl up inside my trainers in embarrassment, even though I knew Amber was pulling my leg.

"Yes, you're a total dark horse!" exclaimed Zoe. "And you have to tell us what our ponies are saying. You just have to!"

Not likely, I thought, deciding I'd have to do some considerable embellishment of characters to make sure that for one thing no one was disappointed and for another I didn't get lynched when they discovered the truth about their darling mounts. I'd learned my lesson there!

"It must be absolutely fantastic being able to hear ponies," sighed Grace, fishing Major out from the bedside drawer and making him canter across her duvet.

"Not always," I said. "Sometimes, they say things I'd rather not hear."

"Like what?" questioned Zoe.

"Oh, er…" That I'd already said too much proved that I hadn't learned any lessons at all! "Oh, the ponies know all sorts of things which we don't."

"You can't prove anything, though," said Ellie slowly, eyeing me. "I mean," she continued, her head on one side, "whatever the ponies tell you, everyone else only has your word that they've said it. What if they don't believe you?"

"If you'd ever heard Pia in action, you'd believe her all right," said Bean loyally. "If it hadn't been for Pia, my Tiffany would probably still be wearing her noseband, and still be head-shaking. She really helped me—and lots of other people at the yard."

I was desperate to change the subject. "Let's plan our midnight feast, instead," I suggested.

"Now you're talking!" said Amber, piling on more lip gloss.

"What are we going to eat?" asked Grace, trotting Major over her pillow and across her bedside table. Major then leapt onto the shelves next to the shower-rooms, soaring across the doorway onto matching shelves on the other side of the room where Ellie sat on her bed concentrating very hard on rummaging through one of her bags. She had her back to Amber, intent on ignoring her. After the spat they'd had at Alex Willard's, Ellie was totally over Amber. The trouble was, Amber hadn't seemed to notice.

"We have to steal some stuff from dinner—and we all need to buy some things from the snack shop," Amber ordered us. The snack shop was a rather glamorous name for a closet in the dining room full of cookies and chocolate bars for sale. There were also postcards and stamps so I'd dutifully sent a postcard to my mom, and another to my dad and Skinny Lynny, telling them what a fabulous time I was having. Mom had phoned me again and told me again how well it was going with the hairless Andy. I wished she wouldn't share so much.

"And it has to be at midnight!" declared Amber.

"Oh, why does it?" moaned Zoe, doing up her sneakers. "I'll never stay awake that long. Why can't we have it as soon as we go to bed?"

"Because it will be a quarter-past-ten feast then, won't it, stupid? I'll set the alarm on my phone. It'll be fantastic!" her sister told her.

"Won't we have to brush our teeth again after?" asked Grace. Major took a giant leap onto Ellie's bed.

"Oh, for goodness sake, you're a bunch of old women!" exclaimed Amber, tearing a brush through her hair.

"No we're not!" argued Bean. "You're right though, it is mandatory. I'm in!"

"And me," I agreed, glad the subject of the feast had replaced that of my pony-whispering powers.

"Me too," said Ellie, deciding to join in at last. "Get your stupid pony off my bed, Grace!"

"Okay, no one say a word at dinner," said Amber. "But

everyone has to wear something with pockets so we can sneak some fruit or cake or something for later."

"Isn't that stealing?" asked Grace doubtfully, holding Major close and daring to glare back at Ellie.

"Of course not," retorted Ellie, "we're just going to eat it later."

"It's deferred consumption," Amber told us.

I put on my vest—it had two big pockets—and hoped Epona wouldn't mind sharing hers with some smuggled edibles.

Our planned food heist ensured plenty of giggling at the table. Mrs. Reeve kept shaking her head and saying, "I don't know what's got into you all tonight," to which Amber replied that we were over excited at having met the amazing, hugely talented, incredibly famous Alex Willard, and did Mrs. Reeve know that she had a real-life celebrity staying with her, Pia Edwards, the Pony Whisperer, as recognized by Alex Willard?

Mrs. Reeve didn't have a clue who I was, so she just smiled indulgently at Amber. "And you're all extra hungry tonight!" she remarked, replacing an empty plate with yet another, full of cookies. Of course, this prompted another spate of giggles from everyone as we smuggled the cookies into our pockets without being spotted. Almost.

"Amber, dear, there's no need to take a cookie for later, you know you can come and get something to eat at any time," Mrs. Reeve said reproachfully, shaking her head.

Amber aimed a grin at her. "You caught me, Mrs. R.!" she

exclaimed, holding up her hands before replacing the cookie on the plate. "I'm so used to doing it at home, I forgot."

"Well, don't put it back!" her sister exclaimed. "No one wants to eat it now your mitts have been all over it. Gross!"

With our pockets bulging, we all tumbled into the living room where Annabelle and Sharon unveiled the evening's entertainment—a karaoke machine.

"Wow!" shouted Zoe, "Karaoke night!" She and Amber did a celebratory high-five with a delighted whoop. I heard Grace groan beside me and sympathized. I wasn't very excited either. I like singing to Drummer, but he always complains and tells me I'm tone deaf, not that he's any better!

But do you know what, Karaoke was a lot of fun! Amber and Zoe stole the show with a duet—they even had a dance to go with it—and everyone clapped like crazy when they'd finished, it was so good. Ellie kept losing her way with the bouncing ball and had to re-start twice. Grace kept stopping and saying she was bad, which was totally annoying. If she'd given it a real try, she'd have been OK. I made a complete mess of my song, but Bean was amazing. She sang really, really well in a very clear voice, and she moved, too, just like a pop star—everyone cheered her on. I suppose her family's musical talents had to rub off on her in some way.

Annabelle and Sharon had a go, too, which was hilarious as Annabelle sang a very long (too long!), sad ballad with a very wobbly voice and a quivering chin, and Sharon belted out a heavy metal number, complete with air guitar and head banging. I could so imagine Sharon at a heavy metal concert, wearing studded leather and black lipstick, puffing on a cigarette.

And then it was time for bed.

CHAPTER 13

"PIA, WAKE UP!" I heard someone say, and I felt them shaking my shoulder.

"Go away!" I said. I didn't want to wake up. I was working for Alex Willard and helping a huge chestnut horse with hang-ups.

"Have some dessert!" the voice whispered again.

Alex receded and the huge chestnut horse morphed into an out-of-focus chocolate brownie.

"You're making me cross-eyed!" I complained, pushing it away.

"Start munching!" ordered Amber. I looked around to see five gray, sleepy faces lit by flashlight.

"Is it midnight?" I asked, yawning.

"Sure is!" said Zoe wickedly. "The witching hour!"

"Oh, that's all I need to think about," said Bean, biting into a banana and chewing.

"I'm not actually very hungry," I said.

"Good," said Ellie, snatching the chocolate brownie from Amber and shoving it in her mouth.

"That's your third!" exclaimed Zoe. "I haven't had one yet!"

"You gotta be quick in this game," Bean said, swallowing. "Who's got the lemonade?"

We munched guiltily. Zoe shone her flashlight round the room, shining it into everyone's eyes and blinding them, and Amber made shadow shapes with her hands as Zoe made the light dance on the wall. We had to guess what the shadows were supposed to be.

"A dinosaur," suggested Grace.

"It's a rabbit, anyone can see that!" said Ellie. "What's the matter with you, Grace?"

"Yup, Mr. Rabbit it is!" confirmed Amber, making another shape with her hands. "Now what's this?"

"Er, looks like a pair of glasses…"

"A tree?"

"Mrs. Rabbit?"

"That's a dinosaur!"

"It's a dog," said Amber, exasperated. "Honestly, it's so obvious."

"I feel a bit sick," mumbled Grace, shaking her head at the offer of more food.

"Oh, please don't be," Zoe said. "This room will smell of vomit for the rest of the week."

"Can we change the subject?" asked Bean. "I vote we all describe our dream ponies."

"Mmmm, good idea!" enthused Amber. "Mine would be a chestnut Arab mare with a blaze and four white legs. She'd let no one else ride her but me, and she'd be brilliant at dressage. Oh, and she'd never get tired so I could ride all day!"

"What would you call her?" asked Grace.

"Sahara. I think that's a fabulous name for an Arab mare."

"Mine would be a black stallion, a top show jumper," said Ellie. "I'd travel the world and compete at all the top shows—Brookdale, the Horse of the Year Show, even the Olympics! We'd win everything."

"What would you call him?" I asked, doing my best to imagine Ellie taking the show jumping world by storm on a glossy black stallion.

"Pride. Ellie's Pride," she replied.

"I've already got my dream pony," Bean said. "Tiffany's just perfect."

"Don't you wish she wasn't so easy to spook?" I asked her. Tiffany was always taking a second look at something.

"No, she's just perfect the way she is," Bean declared, loyally. "She'd be boring if she didn't spook at things. Don't you think Drummer's perfect?"

"Oh yes, I just wish he was a bit bigger so I never grow out of him," I said, imagining Drummer being 16hh. "That would be cool." I pushed the image of Cat with Drummer out of my mind. It refused to go. Pooh!

"What would your dream pony be like, Grace?" asked Bean.

"Shadow."

"Oh, come on, dream a little. What if you could invent the perfect pony?" asked Amber.

"Shadow," repeated Grace. "He is perfect."

"I know what Zoe's dream pony would be," said Amber.

"I can talk for myself, thank you!" Zoe told her. "I'd have a dun gelding, with a tiny white star between his eyes,

121

and I'd call him Dundee, get it? He wouldn't have to be good at anything, as long as I can talk to him and share all my secrets with him."

"That's so nice, Zoe," said Bean. "And that's just how I feel about Tiffany. I always confide in her whenever I'm feeling down about something. It really helps."

I nodded. "Drum was always there for me when my parents got divorced."

"But that's different, you can actually hear what he's saying," said Zoe.

"But ponies just seem to know when you're upset about something, you don't have to be able to actually talk to them," I said. "Having a pony to share your troubles with is just the best thing. You can tell them things you'd never tell another living soul and they always seem to understand."

"That's absolutely right," agreed Bean. "Tiffany and I are a team."

"Oh, I wish I had my own pony!" sighed Grace. "I'm never able to talk to Bobbin at the riding school like you two do with your ponies."

"I thought you didn't want a pony?" I teased.

Grace grinned. "Well, I want one like Shadow."

I thought again how lucky I was to have Drum and suddenly felt tears pricking behind my eyes. I missed him! Did it matter that Cat was looking after him? It was only for a few days and he was still my pony, not hers! I swallowed hard, glad it was so dark in the room and no one could see how emotional I was getting.

"OK!" cried Amber, in an organizational tone. "There's one more thing we have to do during a midnight feast."

"What's that?" asked Grace, stuffing a Fig Newton into her mouth.

"Tell ghost stories!"

"Oh, get lost!" said Bean.

"You're not going to tell that one about the hand again, are you?" asked Zoe in a bored voice.

"Tell us about the hand!" said Grace, bouncing up and down on her bed. Major bounced beside her.

"Puh-leese, no ghost stories, I've been traumatized by séances, thank you!" said Bean.

Totally the wrong thing to say.

"YES!" exclaimed Amber. "That's a much better idea. We'll hold a séance!"

"What's a séance?" asked Grace.

"You call up ghosts, spirits, dead people," explained Bean. "We did one at the yard and it was the scariest thing. There's no way I'm doing that again."

"Did you?" asked Grace breathlessly. "What happened? Did you get anyone?"

"Yeah, we were trying for Dee's granddad, but then we got some lunatic who kept talking about his bad death. It was scary and it freaked me out! I so don't want to do that again!"

"Don't be such a wuss, Bean. That sounds like the best thing! Let's have a show of hands. Who wants to hold a séance?" asked Amber, shining her flashlight under her chin so she looked all spooky.

Grace was up for it—surprisingly. I was astonished. I'd
have thought she'd be the last person to want to hold a séance.
Zoe stuck up her hand and so did I. I felt a tingle go up and
down my spine—I'd sworn I'd never do it again, after the
last experience. But here I was, ready to do it again. Séances
were scary, but that's what made them so compelling.

"I don't want to do it," said Ellie.

"Oh, come on, you're only saying that because I want
to," said Amber. "I'm sorry I was rude to you at Alex
Willard's. The séance will be fun!"

"No," said Ellie quietly.

"Please Ellie, it will be totally awesome," pleaded
Grace, breathlessly.

"I don't want to either," said Bean.

"You don't really believe in them, do you?" Amber
asked. "Oh, come on Bean, come on Ellie, it will be so
cool. What can possibly happen?"

"It's not fair to do it unless everyone wants to," began
Zoe. "Stop bullying them, Amber, you're not in charge."

"If Ellie says she wants to, then I will too," agreed Bean.

"No, I don't want to," said Ellie, shaking her head vigorously.

"Oh, come on, Ellie, pleeeeeese," pleaded Grace.

"You're brave all of a sudden," Ellie said. "Shame you're
not braver when you're riding," she added, spitefully.

"OK, Ellie, we won't then," I said. She was obviously
scared and I knew how that felt. Why bother if it was going
to upset Ellie? Especially if she was going to take it out
on Grace.

"You'll be all right, Ellie, we'll hold your hand," said Amber, so hard-wired into the séance idea that she was determined to ignore anyone else's wishes. "We can write the letters out on some of Grace's drawing paper and use one of the cups in the bathroom. I'll get it."

"NO!" screamed Ellie at the top of her voice, thumping her fists down on the duvet. She screwed up her eyes, huddled her neck down into her shoulders and shouted, "NO, NO, NO, NO, NO, NOOOOO!"

Everyone froze. There was no way Mrs. Reeve couldn't have heard Ellie screaming. The ponies in the field probably heard her. Drummer probably heard her.

"OK, OK, keep your hair on, we'll just tell ghost stories," said Amber, backing off wide-eyed at Ellie's obvious hysteria. "But shhhhhhhh, Ellie, for goodness' sake!"

"It's OK, Ellie, we won't do it, honestly!" Bean said soothingly.

"Trust you, Amber. You never listen to anyone, do you?" hissed Zoe. "It's totally your fault!"

"Oh, lay off, Zo, you just *love* blaming me for everything, don't you!"

"Listen!" hissed Bean. Everyone sat stock still.

"It's Mrs. R.! Quick, lights out, grub away!" ordered Zoe, diving under her duvet and snapping off her flashlight.

We all did the same—even Ellie, who snapped out of her hysterical state quickly enough to stuff the cookies under her pillow. Under the duvet I could hear my heart thumping in time to Mrs. Reeve's footfalls on the stairs.

The door opened and light from the landing flooded into the room. You could have heard a pony cube drop.

"Girls? What's going on? Why aren't you asleep?"

We all stuck our heads out over the duvets. Mrs. Reeve's hair, crinkly from braids and half singed from the barbecue fire, framed her head. She wore a fluffy baby pink robe over some baby blue pajamas and looked like a huge, scary marshmallow. It would have been funny if it hadn't been for Ellie's distress.

"Sorry, Mrs. Reeve," said Amber meekly. "I had a nightmare, a really awful one. Monsters and everything. I'm OK now."

Mrs. Reeve narrowed her eyes. "Are you sure, Amber? You don't strike me as the type of girl to have nightmares. Is there something going on here that I should know about?" She came into the room and visited each bed in turn to check we were OK. When she got to Ellie's bed, she stroked Ellie's hair and asked her very softly whether she was all right, too. Ellie nodded, saying nothing. Then Mrs. Reeve went once more to the door.

"OK, well, I hope you sleep all right now, Amber. Maybe you shouldn't eat so much at dinner time, huh?"

Amber nodded. "I think you're right, Mrs. Reeve. Sorry!"

"Phew, you're really cool, Amber!" said Bean when Mrs. Reeve had gone and the thin line of light under the door snapped out.

"Mrs. Reeve likes you, Ellie," said Grace.

"Yeah," said Zoe, "she always makes a fuss of you. What's that about? Are you related?"

"I'm going to sleep," mumbled Ellie, turning over to face the wall.

"Hey, Ellie, I'm sorry you got so upset about the séance," said Amber. "I didn't realize you felt so strongly about it."

"She told you enough times," Zoe couldn't resist saying. "Only you didn't listen. As usual!"

"Thanks for not giving us all away, Ellie," said Grace.

Ellie said nothing.

Gradually, everyone fell asleep around me. I heard Zoe snoring, heard Bean breathing soundly next to me. I couldn't get to sleep. I thought about Drummer being looked after by Cat. I thought about my mom liking Andy so much. I thought about James. But most of all I thought about the other girls. And when I heard the muffled sound of sobs again I realized they weren't coming from the direction of Grace's bed at all, and they never had. They were coming from Ellie's.

CHAPTER 14

I T'S THE PICNIC RIDE today," Bean declared, examining the timetable pinned up in the dining room.

"I'm so looking forward to that," squealed Grace, peering over Bean's shoulder to see for herself. "I've always wanted to go on a picnic ride!"

"We had a picnic ride at my riding school," Ellie butted in. After last night's hysterics, she was back to being annoying.

"You would have!" mumbled Amber, under her breath.

"It was terrific, the best fun ever," Ellie continued. "Except that the instructor fell off her horse and broke her ankle and I had to ride her horse back. He was huge—almost 17 hands—and no beginner's ride. She said I rode him really well."

"How did she know if she couldn't ride back with you?" asked Amber with a glint in her eye.

"She watched me ride him away—I had to lead the whole ride," Ellie replied.

Bean and I exchanged glances. I don't think any of us believed Ellie. There was no way she was a good enough rider to have done half the things she insisted she'd done. It didn't stack up. We were just glad she seemed to be back to her old self after the midnight feast. Annoying Ellie was much better than hysterical Ellie. Everyone was steering clear of the s-is-for-séance word this morning.

It wasn't long before we were all grooming our ponies for the ride. Everyone's grooming kit was being personalized as the week went on. Bean's kit was starting to look like Tiffany's grooming kit at home—everything just thrown in a heap. Dot's kit, under Zoe's careful eye, was even tidier than when she'd arrived but Amber's was already missing several items. I noticed Major's black plastic head peering out of Grace's grooming tray, wedged between Shadow's body brush and the hoof oil container, and Ellie's was sort of semi-tidy. I looked at Sprout's kit and tidied it up a bit. You never knew, there could be a prize for the tidiest grooming kit, I thought. If so, Zoe was a hot favorite.

Sprout was almost talkative this morning.

"Had a midnight feast last night, did you?" he asked.

"Yes," I said, puzzled. "How can you tell?"

"Are you kidding? You all look like death warmed-over this morning. Zoe's dark circles under her eyes would give a panda a run for its money."

"It was pretty eventful," I told him. "Ellie had a freak out when we wanted to do a séance so that pretty much ended the whole thing."

"I'm hardly surprised," mumbled Sprout. "Poor Ellie, you girls are a tactless bunch."

I yawned. I kinda liked the idea of lying down in the straw and snatching a quick cat nap. I wished I could sleep standing up, like ponies do. Lucky old Shadow, I thought. Then Sprout's words about Ellie sank in and I was just about to ask him what he meant when Bean peered over Sprout's half-door and interrupted my thoughts.

"Can I borrow your curry comb?" she asked, "mine's fallen out into some pony poop—I'll have to clean it with some soap and water."

"Yuck!" I said, fishing around to find Sprout's brush. "Don't drop mine in anything nasty, will you?"

"You make it sound like I did it on purpose," said Bean, stroking Sprout's face. "He's really cute, isn't he?" she said. "Hi, Grace."

"Here," I said, handing Bean Sprout's curry comb. Grace had shuffled up outside the door and was looking at Bean. She looked near to tears and I realized it was the first time since her mom had gone that we'd seen her sucking her hair. Surely she wasn't worried about the picnic ride?

Grace looked at me and then back at Bean, then she beckoned to Bean to follow her. Clearly she considered Bean a more sympathetic confidante. I could live with that.

As Bean followed Grace, I gently sponged Sprout's eyes and nose.

"Thanks," he said.

"You're welcome," I told him, giving him a hug. I was getting really fond of my vacation pony and already dreaded leaving him behind at the end of the week. Wouldn't it be just terrific if I could take him home and have two ponies, I thought. I wondered what Drummer would think of sharing me. He was always whining about having to go riding and schooling, so he could welcome having Sprout to share the load, especially if Cat had stolen his heart...

"Hurry up, girls!" yelled Annabelle. "You're all really slow today. We should be tacked up by now."

"But we're taking extra care because we all want to win the cleanest pony competition," said Zoe.

"You always take aeons and aeons to groom," her sister yelled from Sorrel's stable.

"At least I don't hog the bathroom, dolling myself up," Zoe yelled back.

"Well if you did, you might get a second glance from Patrick Williams!" sneered Amber.

"You leave Patrick Williams out of this!" screamed Zoe.

"Girls, girls!" said Annabelle. "Please start tacking up now."

We all tacked up and mounted, awaiting Annabelle's inspection.

"This is what takes the time," Amber wailed at me as Sorrel pulled a face at Sprout and stamped a hoof. "Annabelle and her wretched clipboard! She's power-mad, that woman!"

"I thought you wanted to win something," I whispered back.

"I thought I did, too but it's such an effort. Zoe's right, I can't be bothered to keep it up all week. I am too impatient—but don't tell her I said so!"

I knew how she felt—cleaning Sprout's gray coat had been a bit of a shock after my bay pony at home. I glanced across at Grace, still sucking her hair. I wondered whether someone had said something to upset her. I hoped it wasn't me.

Finally, Annabelle scuttled off to hide her clipboard in case anyone wanted to spy on how they were doing in the competitions. She then mounted Tailor and led us out of the yard.

"At last!" breathed Amber, nudging Sorrel toward the front. Sorrel was only too willing to oblige, considering the front to be her rightful place. A bit like taking the championship at a show or leading a lap of honor, I thought.

We'd only gone a couple of hundred yards when I could hear Cherokee coming up behind us. Today's complaint seemed to concern his breathing.

"I think I must have RAO—you know, equine asthma," I heard him say to no one in particular. "That's all I need!"

"That's all WE need!" grumbled Sprout.

"I'm definitely wheezy today. Hummmph. Cheeeee. Oh dear. I don't suppose the management will notice. I'll never get the proper treatment. No haylage, no dust-free bedding. I'll be broken-winded before you know it."

"Hey, Crazy McSick-in-the-head, take a day off, will you?" Harry shouted from the back of the ride.

"Not all of us are fortunate to enjoy good health," Cherokee shouted back.

Blissfully unaware of her mount's complaints, Bean steered him over to ride beside me. Looking across, she pulled a face.

"What?" I said. Maybe I had said something to upset Grace. My mind raced but I couldn't remember anything. Oh pooh.

"Something…has…happened," whispered Bean, dramatically.

"What?" I asked again, turning in the saddle.

"Don't look at me!" she hissed. "Just look straight ahead as though we're not talking."

"Oh, OK," I replied, jerking my head round again and staring in front of me in what I hoped was a natural fashion, and doubting it. What was going on? Had Bean suddenly decided she didn't want anyone to look at her? Had she grown a beard or something? I so wanted to glance across to check.

"Something very serious has occurred," whispered Bean.

I looked around at the trees—anywhere but toward her. It could be a beard. I mean, that would be pretty serious, wouldn't it? A very long silence followed. I wondered whether a Bean beard would be blond or some other color. One of the teachers at school had a ginger beard, even though his hair was sort of dirty grayish blond. Mind you, he was a guy. Of course.

"Well?" I said, looking at the sky.

"What?" replied Bean.

Oh no, I thought. Bean always did this. She lost track of what she was talking about and left you on hanging. I dangled for another minute before she deemed it safe to tell me the serious thing that had happened.

"Grace has been the victim of horse rustling," Bean whispered in total seriousness and I struggled to understand what she was saying.

"Major has disappeared," Bean declared. "Grace's pony figurine has been stolen!"

CHAPTER 15

YOU KNOW WHAT THIS means, don't you?" I said to Bean. We'd been riding for over half an hour and this was the first opportunity we'd had to ride together again following a canter, one near-fall from Amber, an emergency concerning Harry's girth which Ellie hadn't tightened and which had been uncharacteristically missed by Sharon (plenty of criticism from Annabelle at that!), and one dropped whip, courtesy of Zoe.

"Well yes, I think I do, but I don't know what you're going to say, so I could be thinking it means one thing and you could be thinking it means something else, but until you say what you're thinking we won't know whether we're thinking the same thing," said Bean without drawing breath.

My head hurt. She'd lost me after about six words. She was back on Planet Bean—a place where no one could reach her.

"Oooo-kaaaay," I said slowly. "How about if I tell you what I think it means?" One of us had to get this ball rolling and if left to Bean we might never get on with it. I just prayed we had both reached the same conclusion.

"I think that the disappearances are all connected,"

I began. Bean nodded furiously in agreement, thank goodness. "And that whoever has stolen Major has also pocketed your gloves."

More nodding. "Exactly!" Bean exclaimed. "But you're missing one vital thing."

"I am?" I asked, a bit miffed that Bean might have thought of something I'd missed.

"Amber's silver charm!"

"You mean...?"

"Yup!" said Bean triumphantly. "Amber's charm must have been stolen, too!"

"That's terrible!" I said. I was finding it difficult to look as though we were just having a chat about our ponies or body brushes or gymkhanas. I mean, this was getting a bit out of hand. It was serious!

"But who did it?" Bean hissed.

"It's obvious who *didn't* do it!" I replied.

"It is?"

"Well, it isn't you, because you had your gloves stolen."

"Right."

"And it can't be Grace or Amber, because they're victims, too."

"Yes, I see that," said Bean, nodding again.

"So it can only be either Zoe or Ellie," I said, feeling like Nancy Drew.

"Or you," added Bean.

"Oh, thanks, I thought my innocence was a given!" I cried, giving her the evil eye.

"I know it wasn't you, obviously, but you have to agree that if we apply your theory logically then you come under suspicion, too," Bean explained.

"I suppose so," I agreed, "but it wasn't me."

"No, I know. That's why I'm telling you and we're discussing it. But then, it could be one of the other victims. I mean, they might be trying to avert suspicion. Maybe, to cover their tracks, they just said they lost something, but really they've got their lost stuff stashed away in a safe place, together with the things they really did steal."

I thought about that. It made sense. I was impressed by Bean's reasoning. "In that case," I said, raising my eyebrows, "you're a suspect, too!"

"Oh, so I am! That sucks!"

"No one," I said dramatically, "is above suspicion!"

"You've seen too many crime dramas," said my friend.

"What are you two whispering about?" asked Zoe.

We both jumped about a mile in the air. I ask you, could we have looked any more guilty?

"Who's going to win the tidiest-stable competition," I lied, hoping I wasn't going red.

Wrong thing to say. Zoe went off about how she was sure she was in the running, and that Amber didn't stand a chance and neither did Grace or Ellie because of their inexperience—had we seen the bed in Harry's stable, it was a disgrace—and she wasn't one to brag but Dot's stable was far and away cleaner than everyone else's stables—even mine and Bean's, even though mine was quite good. I gave her a forced smile in sarcastic gratitude, and she rode off, having said her piece.

"She's such a bore when it comes to anything to do with competitions," sighed Bean, who couldn't be bothered with it all. "She's a trainee Annabelle."

"So who do you think it is, then?" I whispered, desperate to get back to solving the crime wave.

"Who do I think is what?" asked Bean.

It only took a minor distraction to make Bean lose the thread of a conversation. I couldn't remind her about what we'd been talking about just then because we all had an awesome canter along some sandy tracks by a stream and then, when we pulled up at the end, Annabelle led the way down the bank and all the ponies enjoyed a paddle, putting their heads down to drink from the clear water. All except for Cherokee, that is, who stood on the bank snorting, despite Bean's efforts to make him go in.

"You'll never do it," said Sharon, shaking her head. "No one ever has yet. He's too much of a wuss."

"This is great fun, I LOVE water!" yelled Harry, pawing at the stream and splashing everyone.

"Stop that!" said Sorrel. "My mane goes frizzy when it's wet!"

"Don't let Dot-2-Dot stand still, Zoe, she likes to roll in water," Annabelle warned. "Keep her moving and if she paws at the ground, ride her out immediately!"

"Oh, I hope she goes down, I'll laugh my socks off!" Amber cried, urging Sorrel in front of the Appaloosa, preventing Zoe from moving anywhere.

"Get out of the way, Amber!" shouted Zoe.

"No way, I want to see her drop you in the water!" laughed her sister.

"Amber, MOVE!" screamed Annabelle. But it was too late. Dot pawed at the water and sank to her knees, threatening to roll onto her side. Flapping her feet out of her stirrups in a panic, Zoe let out a piercing shriek, causing a mass evacuation of birds from the surrounding bushes. Shouting at Zoe to kick Dot on, Annabelle steered Tailor over toward her and gave Dot's spotty backside a loud thwack with her whip. Leaping up again, Dot veered away from Tailor and Zoe slid off, hitting the water with a splash and a gasp.

Amber screamed with laughter and everyone else couldn't help giggling. It was hysterical seeing Zoe sitting in the water spluttering and gasping with the shock of the cold water, Dot looking down at her as though she was crazy.

"That's not fair—I wanted to lie in the water!" Dot moaned. "How come it's all right for her to sit in it, but not me?"

"Because, Empty, dear, you'll break your saddle tree, you dummy!" explained Harry.

"I don't know why you'd want to sit in that water," Cherokee called from the bank. "It's cold and wet and you could catch your death. You never know what's crawled in and died in it. And even fish poop you know. And ducks. You wouldn't catch me going anywhere near it! Water's teeming with germs."

"D'you know what, Cherokee?" said Harry. "One day you're going to wake up and realize that you were so busy avoiding things all through your life that nothing actually happened during it and you missed it all. What a waste that will be!"

"Dung heaps!" retorted Cherokee.

"Double dung heaps to you!" replied Harry, yawning.

"I think we'll have our picnic here," announced Annabelle, unaware of the raging equine argument. "It will give Zoe a chance to dry out."

Riding out of the stream we all dismounted, ran up our stirrups and loosened the girths, tying the ponies by their harnesses to string Sharon wrapped round the trees. Sharon and Annabelle distributed the picnic from their saddlebags and backpacks: sausage rolls; chicken, cheese and pickle and egg salad sandwiches; chips; cereal bars; apples and bananas; and a slice of chocolate cream pie in plastic cartons for everyone. Of course, the apples found their way into the ponies' mouths, but we fell upon the rest and were soon munching away.

"Ew, what's that awful smell?" said Ellie, wrinkling up her nose and cautiously sniffing her sandwich.

"I can smell something, too," I said, looking at the ground in case we'd sat in fox poop.

"Oh, it's you, Zoe, you reek!" shrieked Amber, waving her hand in front of her face.

Zoe sniffed her T-shirt. "Oh, it is me," she wailed. "It's this stinky river water!"

Everyone moved away from smelly Zoe, which gave Bean and me the perfect excuse to sit ever-so-slightly apart from the others so we could continue our crime wave discussion.

"Is Grace going to tell Annabelle about Major?" I asked.

"I think she'll have to," whispered Bean. "I mean, it's just not right, someone stealing her pony. It's just mean."

"Is she sure she hasn't just lost him?" I asked. I don't know why—I mean, there was Bean's gloves and Amber's necklace to take into account so it was fairly obvious someone was helping themselves. But the thought of one of us stealing stuff was just too horrible to consider. I felt for Epona in my pocket again. What if someone took her? What would I do then? Shuddering, I knew I couldn't let her out of my sight, not for a second.

I looked around at my fellow vacationers. Who could possibly have stolen the items? Who hadn't had anything stolen?

Ellie? I couldn't take to Ellie. She just didn't do anything to make you like her, but that was no real basis for suspicion. You couldn't accuse someone just because you didn't like them much.

Zoe? She might have taken Amber's silver charm out of spite—there was certainly no love lost between the two sisters. But why would she take Bean's gloves and Grace's pony figurine as well?

Amber? Losing Silver could be a ploy to throw everyone off the scent; Amber was certainly clever enough to think of that, but I somehow couldn't picture Amber with

141

Major—she'd been really nice to Grace. I didn't want it to be Amber, I liked her. I felt a pang of guilt. I wanted it to be Ellie because I didn't like her. That was hardly fair.

It wasn't Bean. It just wasn't.

Grace? No, not Grace, she was too upset about Major for her to be faking it. But then, I thought, why couldn't it be Grace? Her mother bullied her and there was no doubt she had hang-ups. Maybe it was her way of coping with it all, collecting things other people held valuable, or getting someone else into trouble by accusations.

I shuddered again.

"What's the matter, Pia?" I looked up to see Annabelle looking thoughtfully at me.

"Oh, nothing!" I replied, a bit too heartily. Keep this up, I thought to myself, and when Grace does the big reveal, I'll be the number one suspect. How great would that be? Luckily, Annabelle's attention was distracted by something else. Unluckily, it was Grace, who couldn't hold it any longer, and had started to cry.

Putting her arm around her, Annabelle steered Grace over to the shade of an oak tree, and we all pretended not to watch them having a chat. Poor Grace gulped a lot, dabbing at her eyes with a paper napkin and sucking her hair, and we could see Annabelle stroking the hair off her face and nodding.

"What's going on?" Sharon asked us. "Have you girls been horrible to her?"

We all shook our heads and I hoped I didn't look guilty.

If I did, it was only because I knew why Grace was crying, not because I was the cause of it.

Eventually, they came back. Grace's eyes were red and sore and Annabelle held her arm protectively round her shoulders.

"I need to talk to you all," Annabelle said in a serious tone.

I glanced at everyone. Did Ellie look shifty? Was that anxiety I could detect on Zoe's face? Did Amber look less confident than usual?

"Grace has mislaid her pony figurine," Annabelle said carefully. "She last saw it in the yard this morning, and it may have fallen from her grooming kit. If anyone has seen it, or has it with them, perhaps you would let us know now because, as you can see, it means a lot to Grace and she is very upset at having lost it."

Everyone looked at each other. No one spoke. No one put their hand in their pocket and pulled out Major with an apologetic smile. I exchanged confused glances with Bean. Major had been stolen, not lost, so why was Annabelle suggesting he'd been mislaid? And then, suddenly, I clicked. Making accusations about stealing probably wasn't the best thing to do. Better to give whoever had stolen Major the opportunity to return him without any unpleasantness. A bit like the tried-and-tested formula 'I'm going to close my eyes and count to ten', to give whoever took the object the chance to return it, and we'll say no more about it—only Annabelle didn't know about Bean's missing gloves, and she still thought Amber had lost her necklace out riding.

After an awkward few, very silent, seconds, Annabelle spoke again. "We'll all help you to have a really good look for your figurine when we get back to the yard, Grace. I'm sure it will turn up there. There are plenty of places for it to hide!"

Another opportunity for whoever took Major to 'find' him, I thought. Clever Annabelle.

We bridled the ponies and mounted in sober mood.

Bean asked Zoe whether she'd dried out. Zoe put her hand on her backside. "Not quite, I'm still damp, thanks to my loving sister!" she glowered at Amber, who stuck her tongue out at her as she gathered up Sorrel's reins.

"And you still reek!" Amber said.

Bean steered Cherokee over to Sprout's side. "Do you think Major will turn up?" she whispered to me.

"Don't know, he might," I replied, checking my girth.

"I bet he doesn't," Bean said, frowning. "Who knows what will go missing next?"

I turned Sprout so that no one could see me transfer Epona from my vest pocket to the zipped pocket in my jodhpurs, where I could feel her against my hip bone. She dug in a bit and I would probably get a bruise, but I wanted her close, where I could feel her. No one was going to steal Epona away from me, I decided. I'd die if I lost her now.

CHAPTER 16

I'VE SEEN IT! I know who's winning what!" Amber declared.

"You are so full of It," her sister replied, looking bored. We were in the chill-out room, waiting for the ponies to digest their feed. It was almost time for our lesson.

"What are you two talking about?" asked Bean, flicking through one of the many pony books lying around.

"The clipboard. Annabelle's bible. I've seen it and you, Zoe, are not going to win anything. Not a thing. Ha! All that effort for nothing!"

"You're lying—that clipboard is practically welded to Annabelle's arm and when it's not, it's under lock and key. You've seen diddly-squat," Zoe sneered, looking down her nose at her sister. "And you just don't get it, do you? I don't groom and clean tack so I can win things, I do it because I like to see Dot-2-Dot looking her best and wearing nice clean tack. I don't want to be a scruff-bag, like you."

"Who is winning?" asked Grace.

"Oooh, can't say," replied Amber, forming her mouth into an O shape and looking at Grace all wide-eyed. "Unless you pay me—I know you've got some Mounds bars in your bedside table, Grace. I might be able to let you know more if one of those was to come my way."

"That's blackmail!" declared Bean.

"Is it? I thought it was extortion," said Amber. "Anyway, I'm only joking."

"I told you, she hasn't seen the clipboard," yawned Zoe.

"Oh, I have, I was joking about the Mounds bars," said Amber, grinning. "Although of course, if you wanted to share them out, Grace, I wouldn't say no. I'll help you take another look for Major if you like."

At the mention of her missing figurine, Grace gulped.

"Oh, you are tactless, Amber," Zoe said, putting her arm round Grace. "Come on Grace, I'll help you get Shadow ready for the lesson. Take no notice of Miss Foot-in-mouth over there."

"What?" asked Amber, a picture of innocence. "I was trying to help."

Bean and I hung back as the others drifted out to tack up again.

"I've been thinking," said Bean in her best detective voice. "You're going to have to get the ponies involved."

"What makes you think they know anything?" I asked.

"Because my gloves disappeared in the yard. Major went AWOL from the yard. One of the ponies may have seen something. Or…" Bean's eyebrows almost met over her nose as she screwed up her face in concentration. "… the thief may even have confided in her pony. Have you heard them talking about it?"

"No, I haven't. When did you figure all this out?" I said. Bean was constantly surprising me—she didn't get

146

the most basic of concepts, living on Planet Bean for much of the time, but then she came out with all these theories. Clearly, she was on another level. Perhaps it was her artistic side—coming out in a different way to the rest of her family, and to normal people.

"I told you, I've been thinking," she said. I wondered just how smart Bean would be if she did more of it. "Plus," she added, looking around, "did you hear Amber say she knew Grace had Mounds bars in her bedside cabinet?"

"Yes, I did!"

"How did she know that? Has she been snooping—does she know what everyone has in their bedside cabinet?" asked Bean.

I felt a shiver run up and down my spine. "Oh, we have to get this figured out. I'll ask Sprout," I said. I felt a bit stupid—I should have thought about asking the ponies. I was just a bit preoccupied with worrying about how Drum was getting on with Cat. How dumb was I?

I wasted no time. I tacked up Sprout in record time and then, checking that everyone else was busy adjusting throatlashes, tightening girths and strapping hats to their heads or, in Zoe's case, standing in front of Dot-2-Dot and tweaking her noseband and browband until they were dead straight and parallel, I told Sprout I needed his help with something mega important.

"I know, I know, you want to win the jumping tomorrow," he said with a snort.

"No, nothing like that—although I wouldn't say no, obviously. No, I need your help with some detective work."

"Explain."

So I did. I told him about Amber's silver charm and Bean's gloves and Grace's figurine, Major. I explained how upset Grace was, and how things could get totally out of hand if anything else went missing. "Because at the moment," I told him, "only Major is officially stolen—even though Annabelle is playing it down. Bean hasn't kicked up about her gloves and Amber still thinks she lost her silver charm, but I don't think that's the case. I think everything has been taken by someone, as yet unknown. And that's where you and the other ponies come in," I finished.

"You want me to rat on the thief."

"Well, yes. Why wouldn't you? I mean, someone is taking things which are not theirs. Someone is upsetting the people who have had things taken. Someone," I concluded dramatically, "needs to be stopped!"

Sprout said nothing.

I heard Annabelle shouting at us to hurry up. "Well?" I asked Sprout. "Do you know who the culprit is? Can you tell me so we can get this figured out and cheer up poor Grace? She's so upset about Major, and who knows what else might go missing! I mean, it's horrible to steal things."

"Let me get back to you on that," said my vacation pony.

"Get back to me?" I hissed. "Do you know who it is, or not?"

"I need to have a word," he replied.

"Who with?"

"Look, it isn't as easy as all that. You sound very judgmental about the person who's taken these things," Sprout said, shifting his weight from one front hoof to the other.

"Well, yes, I am. I mean, stealing! It just isn't right!"

"There may be underlying factors as yet unknown to you," said Sprout. "Factors which make this case less about stealing and more about—well, I've said too much. Leave it with me and, as I say, I'll get back to you. It isn't up to me. Come on, let's get this lesson over with."

I had to wait until the end of the lesson when we were waiting our turn to jump before I could tell Bean. I nudged Sprout up beside Cherokee who was grumbling about the flies. I knew Sprout could hear me, and hoped he'd pick up on the disappointment in my voice. And Bean's.

"What underlying factors?" she asked.

I shrugged my shoulders. "Dunno!"

"When is he getting back to you?"

"Dunno that either. When do you think you'll be getting back to me, Sprout?" I whispered.

"Come to the field later, I may be able to tell you more then," Sprout said out of the corner of his mouth. I don't know why—unless he didn't want the other ponies to hear.

I would have relayed this back to Bean, only it was her turn to jump and I had to wait for her to return. And then it was my turn and we managed a clear round. I made a lot of Sprout, hoping it would help our case. I told Bean as we put our tack away.

"Do you think underlying factors could include some kind of illness?" asked Bean.

"Or maybe the person is insane. Insanity could be an underlying factor."

"I don't get it," said Bean. "Stealing is stealing. And I want my gloves back—the thought of someone else wearing them makes me crazy!"

"Mmmm. Let's hope the ponies decide to spill the beans. Sorry—that sounds funny 'cause of your name!"

"Oh ha, ha!" Bean replied, her voice heavy with sarcasm. "Like I haven't heard that one before."

And then a thought whooshed into my head, a thought which hadn't occurred to me before, but could explain the ponies' reluctance to tell us anything. "Oh!" I said, staring into space as the thought developed, galloping on like a runaway horse.

"What?" asked Bean. "You look like you've swallowed a fly."

"What if?" I began, trying to figure out my thoughts as I relayed them to Bean, "the thief isn't one of us?"

"Huh?"

"What if it's Annabelle. Or Sharon?"

Bean let out a low whistle. I wish I could do that. Everyone else seems to be able to whistle except me.

"But Sharon went to look for Amber's silver charm Oh. Oh, I see," said Bean, frowning. "Maybe she found it. Maybe she already had it!"

"Your gloves were expensive. You'll be gone after this

week and Sharon—or Annabelle, she wears good stuff—
could wear them without arousing suspicion. Maybe that's
why Sprout wouldn't tell us. I mean, Annabelle and Sharon
are part of High Grove Farm."

"We're forgetting Major," said Bean. "Why would they
steal Major? Can you imagine Annabelle or Sharon playing
with toy ponies when we all go home?"

"They might like it for their niece, or little sister, I don't
know." The Major part didn't stack up, which annoyed me.

"We can't discount them," Bean said. "We can't discount anyone."

Of course, getting away from everyone else once we had
turned the ponies out and cleaned tack proved impossible.
We weren't supposed to amuse ourselves, but be part of the
constant, full-on vacation package at High Grove Farm.
First it was dinner—which we had no intention of missing.
Then Annabelle and Sharon had a trivia night all planned.

"Form two teams," Annabelle ordered, clipboard firmly
in hand.

"Dibs on being with Bean!" yelled Amber. "She won the
holiday by winning the quiz in *Pony* mag, so she's bound
to be brilliant!"

"OK!" agreed Bean, winking at me as I had answered
most of the questions. Grace joined Amber and Bean
to form team A, and Zoe, Ellie and I made up team B.
Questions ranged from mega easy—name three British
native pony breeds, for example—to totally impossible.
No one knew the name of Napoleon's horse, or the color

of the horses used by the Canadian Mounted Police, or the name of the 14.2hh pony that won Great Britain a silver medal for show jumping in the 1968 Olympic Games (Marengo, black and Stroller, if you're interested). It was a fun quiz, though, and Team A won by only two points, giving Amber and Zoe something else to argue about. By the time the quiz had finished and we'd all had some cake and drinks it was dark outside and time for bed.

"What are we going to do?" I asked Bean as we went up the stairs.

"We'll have to sneak out when the others are asleep," she said.

"What?"

"We have to keep our rendezvous with Sprout. It's the only way we'll find out. You're not scared, are you?"

"Er, yes, actually. Plus, the others might wake up!"

"We'll have to be totally like little mice. All quiet and tiptoe-y."

Everyone seemed to take forever to go to sleep. Amber wanted to talk about the gymkhana tomorrow and Ellie insisted that she had a good chance of winning something. Eventually, one by one, the others drifted off. I dreaded hearing the sounds of crying—I thought Grace might stay awake worrying about Major—but she was soon breathing rhythmically, like everyone else. Except Zoe. She really did snore!

"Ready?" whispered Bean.

I wasn't. I was warm and cozy in bed.

Have you ever tried to creep around quietly when someone else is sleeping in the same room? Honestly, it's like everything makes extra-loud noises on purpose. Floorboards suddenly decide to creak, bedsprings ping, doors whine. Everything you do seems to make far more noise than it does in the daytime—because it's the only noise you can hear, no one else is talking or rustling or making awake, I'm-in-the-room noises. Even pulling on jodhpurs and a sweater seemed to make more noise than a box of monkeys—a box of monkeys with drums and whistles. I was sure we'd woken Zoe up at one point, but then after a couple of gurgles, she was off again, snoring.

Bean and I let ourselves out of the bedroom and on to the creaking wooden floorboards on the landing. Tiptoeing down the stairs in our bare feet, holding our breath and our boots, we reached the hallway and fumbled our way toward the back door.

Suddenly, something let out a loud, unearthly shriek and shot past me, brushing my legs. I froze, my heart stopping in total dread. It had to be a ghost. Some terrible spirit we'd disturbed—the spirit of High Grove Farm which had been wandering about all the time we'd been asleep upstairs, blissfully unaware that the place was haunted. Why on earth had we thought a séance would be fun? I mean, toying with the occult was such a totally bad, *bad* idea; of course these old places had ghosts, evil, vindictive spirits intent on…

"I think I just stood on Soot," Bean whispered, cutting

short my rambling mind. It wasn't enough to stop my heart thudding. Surely everyone in the house could hear that?

"Do you think," I whispered, "you could look where you're putting your feet from now on? I almost died of fright."

"Well, I would if I could see anything. It's pitch black in here, in case you hadn't noticed."

"Serves Soot right," I replied, too shaken to be charitable. "A black cat in the dark is just asking to be stepped on."

We let ourselves out of the door, pulled on our jodhpur boots and headed off past the yard to the ponies' field. A huge silvery moon hung in the sky like a beacon. I had no idea a moon could be so bright—it threw shadows from trees and the yard like the sun does, only in shades of black, dark black and even darker black. Everything was quiet and still, the only sound we could hear was the faint rustling of leaves as the trees swayed in the night breeze. The air was cold and I shivered in my sweater. It wasn't enough to keep me warm in the night air.

Climbing over the field gate we approached the ponies, grouped together by the trough. I could make out Harry's cobby frame and Sorrel's slender build. In the gloom their colors were muted, as though filmed in black-and-white. I could feel my heart thudding again. Would the ponies tell us what we wanted to know? Who the thief was? I shivered. Now we were there, I wasn't sure I really wanted to know.

CHAPTER 17

WHAT DO YOU INTEND to do if we tell you what you want to know?" Sprout asked me. I gulped. Surround by the ponies, I felt as though we'd done something wrong and the ponies were judging us. It was the weirdest sensation. From Sprout's serious tone, it was as though the ponies were on the side of the thief. It was all very strange. I decided to consult Bean—mainly because she was tugging at my sleeve and demanding I tell her what was going on.

"Who is it?" she whispered.

"I don't know yet. They want to know what we're going to do if they tell us," I explained.

"Oh. I don't know. I just want my gloves back. We want Grace to get Major back and for Amber to get her silver charm back. That's all."

I turned to Sprout. He and Shadow were the easiest ponies to see in the gloom and they both gleamed silver in the moonlight. Harry and Cherokee's white patches looked like floating lava lamp blobs, suspended eerily in mid-air. I could see Dot-2-Dot quite clearly—her spots looked like she was full of holes—but Sorrel looked sort of dark gray.

"The thing is," interrupted Harry, pushing his way

past Sprout and standing in front of me, "we need you to understand that the person behind all this thievin' may have problems, issues like, that you don't know about."

"Is it Grace?" I said. "I know she has problems with her mom. We don't want to upset her but it isn't right that other people have to suffer. Bean wants her gloves back, and Amber's silver charm is valuable."

"Why would it be Grace?" asked Bean.

"They say the thief has issues," I explained.

"Has she got a cold?"

"What?"

"What do tissues have to do with anything?"

"Not tissues, issues!" I hissed.

"Well, I've got issues, we've all got issues," muttered Bean moodily. "I don't take my issues out on other people by stealing their stuff!"

"You're not helping," I said.

"Sorry. Only we could all use issues as an excuse!"

"What I am trying to explain," Harry continued, "is that just 'cause a person appears to be a pain in the tail, appears not to fit in, appears to behave in a way that puts people against them, it doesn't mean they don't have a reason to behave that way."

"Sometimes a person is so desperate for friends, their attempts to win people over have the very opposite effect," explained Sprout, not explaining at all. "It's a cry for help."

I sighed. All this dancing around the issue was making me very confused.

"Why don't you just explain everything to us?" I suggested. "Then we might understand what you mean. I don't understand anything at the moment."

"We need you to promise not to be judgmental," Harry said solemnly. "You must promise not to reveal the secret we tell you tonight—about the thief."

I relayed it all to Bean and we both nodded, agreeing to the terms. I felt a bit spooked—what secret were we going to learn and did we really want to know it?

Harry cleared his throat. Bean tugged at my sleeve. "What's he saying?" she asked earnestly.

"Nothing yet," I told her. If I was going to translate every word we would be here all night. I half-wished I'd come alone, but knew I'd never have made it past the front door without some moral support. I was too much of a wuss.

"Do you know that people's behavior is often a result of how other people treat them?" Harry asked. "And that confident, attractive people get a positive reaction from others, which in turn has a snowball effect, making them even more confident and attractive?"

I repeated it to Bean and I could hear her nodding furiously. She obviously understood more than I did. I sort of understood. It was a bit like my mom—once she'd had her makeover and felt confident, she had acted more confidently. Since then, she'd had loads of boyfriends. They hadn't wanted to know when she'd shuffled around feeling sorry for herself. An image of a shiny, hairless man with my mom leapt uninvited into my mind. I shook it out. Not the right time to be focusing on that!

"Think of the person on this holiday everyone has been most negative about—you two included," Harry told us. I started to feel uncomfortable. We'd come to discover the thief, not be psychoanalyzed. I translated to Bean. I was beginning to feel like one of those interpreters at the United Nations, only I couldn't translate at the same time as Harry spoke.

"Oh dear" mumbled Bean. "I haven't been very nice to Ellie—but she's so..."

"Yes, I know," I interrupted her. "She's so annoying."

"So you get my point," Harry said.

"What's that got to do with the stolen—oh, are you telling us that Ellie is the culprit?"

Bean grabbed my arm. "Ellie? Really?"

I saw Harry's head nod in the gloom. "I saw Ellie lift Bean's gloves from the bench and Sorrel saw her take Major from Grace's grooming kit. She may or may not have Amber's silver charm. We haven't seen her with it."

"But why?" I asked. "She's always telling us she's got this and that, that she's getting a super-duper pony and going on and on about how good a rider she is, even though she's not. Why?"

"Maybe she's trying to impress you all. It could be she feels left out and is desperately trying to be included," suggested Sprout.

"There is another reason," said Harry.

"Go on," I said after repeating what Sprout had told me to my impatient accomplice.

"Ellie has been sent here by her father in an effort to help her get over something tragic that has happened in her life," Harry said solemnly.

I held my breath, remembering Ellie crying in the night. What Harry said next sent a shiver through my heart and a chill down my spine.

"Ellie has recently lost her mother. She died just two months ago."

I thought of Ellie's terror when we'd wanted to hold a séance—no wonder, given her circumstances. I remembered how she'd reacted at the barbecue when we'd all gone on about our moms. We'd been cruel without even knowing it—whining and complaining about our own moms. I couldn't even imagine how Ellie must be feeling.

I gulped. I so didn't want to tell Bean. The words stuck in my throat. Poor Ellie. I thought of all the times I'd decided she was lying about her prowess as a rider, of all the times she'd got on my nerves, making her try harder to get attention. We hadn't given her a chance. Not really. We hadn't been very nice to her and we hadn't bothered to wonder whether there was a reason why she behaved like she did.

I managed to tell Bean in hushed tones. I felt it ought to be whispered. I heard her catch her breath.

"Our riders sometimes confide in us," Harry said. "If they haven't a pony of their own, they'll often talk to us."

"We're happy to help," said Shadow, kind as ever. "They're our responsibility for a week so we like to do what we can."

"We take our jobs very seriously, you know, despite our arguments and grumbles," Sorrel added. "It doesn't just stop at the riding."

I thought of Drummer at home. I'd lost count of the number of times I'd leaned on his bay neck and told him my troubles. When Mom and Dad had got divorced, when we had moved, when things weren't going right at school—even when my pet guinea-pig had died, Drum had been there. Even way before I could hear him talk back to me he had just chewed on his hay, sympathetic to my woes, always there for me.

Harry spoke again: "So you see, you can't let Ellie know you know about her mother because then she would know I had betrayed her confidence. It is only because of special circumstances that I am telling you this. You need to understand why she stole those things."

"But what's the connection?" I asked, still unsure.

"I dunno, I'm a pony. I just know that the two are linked in some way. Ask a psychiatrist if you want to know why. I'm just telling you what happened."

"How can we get this sorted out?" asked Bean. "What do they recommend?"

I asked Harry. "I don't know that either," he said. "You wanted to know who was stealing, and now you do. Just don't put me in the middle of what you decide to do. Now you'll have to excuse us, we have a very important meeting concerning our work tomorrow."

"Hold on..." I began.

"What?" asked Harry.

"You all make fun of Dot-2-Dot. Isn't that the same thing?" I asked.

"That's just banter," said Harry. "We always stick together in the end. Dot's one of us, one of our team. Isn't that right, Dot?"

"Oh yes," agreed Dot. "Er, what?"

Bean and I crept back to the house in silence, both feeling guilty about the way we'd treated Ellie.

"You just never know about people, do you?" whispered Bean as we inched open the back door and eased into the hallway.

"Shhhh!" I said, terrified of being caught.

"I think you should confront Ellie," Bean said.

"Why me?"

"Because you can say you know she stole the stuff because the ponies told you."

"Harry asked us not to tell on him!"

"I know, but couldn't you say you overheard Sprout talking to Cherokee and keep Harry out of it? If you say you *overheard*, rather than *they told you*, all the ponies are in the clear."

"Mmmm," I mumbled, "I suppose." I didn't like the sound of it. That was the trouble with the whole pony-whispering thing, it meant I had to do things I didn't especially want to do, simply by default.

I don't know how Bean and I managed to get undressed and in bed without waking anyone else up but we did. I stayed awake for ages, thinking and wondering and dreading confronting Ellie. But I knew I had to do it, and the next day, too. I had to get the silver charm, gloves, and pony back to their rightful owners before the end of the vacation.

CHAPTER 18

"I CAN'T WAIT FOR THE jumping!" exclaimed Grace, absentmindedly flicking the braids on Shadow's withers.

"I bet you never thought you'd say that!" laughed Amber. "You're a completely different Grace to the one who arrived here on Monday."

"Yes," said Grace, grinning from ear to ear, "I am, aren't I? And it's all because of Shadow. I wish I didn't have to leave him behind. I wish he could come home with me, I love him so much." Shadow didn't bother to open his eyes at Grace's declaration. Every spare moment was a dozing opportunity not to be missed.

The final day's gymkhana turned out to be great fun. All the parents turned up to watch, sitting on chairs outside the school. I'd been relieved when I'd seen my mom turn up alone, I'd been terrified she'd bring that Andy guy.

"Oh, I'm not seeing him anymore," she'd said when I quizzed her. "He's far too intense. I couldn't handle it."

So much for him being The One, I thought, vowing never to waste time worrying about Mom's boyfriends in the future. She sat between Bean's arty mom, with whom she had traveled down, and Grace's scary mom, who was looking intently for improvement in her daughter's riding.

Zoe and Amber's parents were really nice—their mom was mega glamorous with lots of hair—and had given all the ponies sugar lumps as soon as they arrived, which had caused uproar as the ponies got pretty demanding, and Annabelle had gotten very uptight, which was funny.

Bean and I had exchanged glances when Ellie's dad arrived. Ellie had thrown herself at him and they'd hugged for a long time. He was a nice-looking man with glasses and he looked just like anyone's dad, only really, really tired. It had been bad enough when my parents got divorced but at least I still saw my dad. I couldn't imagine how it would be if he'd died and I knew I would never, ever see him again. How could Ellie and her dad cope with missing her mom?

"How are we going to get Grace's mom to buy her Shadow?" Bean asked me as we watched Grace, Amber and Ellie complete their heat of the barrel race.

"Oh, I don't know, I've had enough excitement for one day," I whispered back. "I'm emotionally drained."

"Oh puh-leese, you're such a drama-queen!" Bean said, rolling her eyes.

"What?"

"You only had to have a quiet word with Ellie and she's given everything back. What's the big deal?"

The big deal was, well, a *big deal* for me. I hadn't been looking forward to speaking to Ellie but in the end, it hadn't been too bad, I suppose. I'd cornered her in the yard when everyone was braiding their ponies hair and told her I'd overheard the ponies talking and knew she'd taken the silver charm, the gloves, and Major. She'd turned white and then admitted it. Which was a huge relief. I mean, what if she'd denied it? I didn't have a back-up plan. But Ellie had cried a bit once she'd come clean, especially when she realized I wasn't going to tell anyone else, or be horrible to her. So we worked out a way for her to leave the things where they could be found so that she didn't have to confess or explain. I'd made a real effort to be nice to her and she had been so grateful that I was willing to help her. She was a lot easier to like when she wasn't bragging.

And it had worked. Sharon found Major in the feed room, sticking out of the carrot sack. Bean's gloves appeared draped over Cherokee's saddle and Amber discovered her silver charm in the pocket of her favorite pink vest. Which wasn't a good idea—she immediately accused Zoe of having hidden it there. Zoe insisted she hadn't looked properly in the first place and it had been there all the time, and so it went on, and on, and on.

"Bad move!" Bean had said. "Why couldn't Ellie have stuffed it in Amber's suitcase? That way, she'd have found Silver when she got home, and we'd have been spared the bickering!"

The person having the most fun on this last day appeared to be Annabelle. Dressed in a lemon shirt and very expensive designer breeches she brandished her clipboard and blew her whistle, which she used to start the races. And to silence everyone when she wanted to say something. And to get Sharon's attention. And if she saw anyone doing anything she thought we shouldn't be doing—like when

Amber, in a moment of insanity, thought it would be a good idea to dismount from Sorrel by easing herself over the cantle of the saddle, sliding back and slipping off her rump, facing her tail.

"What am I now, a circus pony?" Sorrel had said, wide-eyed and indignant.

"My braids are too tight. It's like someone's tweaking three hairs in each one. Ouch! Whoever braided me must have been trained by monkeys," I heard Cherokee complain.

Sharon, of course, did all the hard work—running around with gymkhana props, heaving jumps back and forth and clearing the school. Annabelle just gave out orders and looked glamorous. Amber and Zoe's dad couldn't stop looking at her—and their mom kept nudging him, laughing and rolling her eyes.

The gymkhana was great fun—even the ponies stopped complaining and joined in enthusiastically and everyone won something. Amber won the musical sacks (like musical chairs but with horses!), Ellie the barrel race and Zoe somehow managed to coax Dot first past the winning post in the walk, trot and canter race. Cherokee stopped whining long enough to carry Bean to victory in the flag race and Sprout was an absolute star in the stepping stone race, enabling me to win the blue ribbon.

All the parents cheered from the sidelines and Mrs. Reeve put on a big spread for everyone (she kept dabbing her eyes with a hanky and saying she always missed her girls when they went home) between the gymkhana and prize giving and the final event—the eagerly awaited show jumping. Zoe carried off the prizes for both the cleanest tack and best-kept stable competitions, and Ellie took the grooming prize—because she'd improved so much over the week, Annabelle said.

You'll never guess who won the jumping. Grace! I know, no one else could believe it either. I thought I was in the running until the very last jump—we met it all wrong and Sprout dropped a hind toe on the pole, bringing it crashing down. But what was more surprising than Grace winning (you should have seen the look on her face as Shadow carefully heaved himself over the last and through the finish) was that the result rendered Grace's mom speechless for at least three seconds.

"She has to buy Shadow now!" enthused Bean.

When the time came for us to say good-bye to our ponies, there wasn't a dry eye in the house.

"I wish you could come home with me," I whispered to Sprout. "I'm so going to miss you."

"Only for as long as it takes you to get home and be reunited with that Drummer pony you keep going on about," Sprout said. "Besides, I'll have another rider next week."

"Do you mind not having your own person?" I asked him.

"Not really—it's part of the job. It's fun here with the others, we have lots of laughs—but you know that, being a pony whisperer. I'm going to miss Harry, though."

"Miss Harry? Why? Where's he going?"

"Haz is going to be Ellie's pony. It's all settled with Mrs. Reeve."

"No!" I said stunned. "Is Harry OK with that?"

"Thrilled. He's looking forward to a new challenge. He never really got over losing his old owner. He'll love being someone's only pony again."

I imagined Ellie with Harry. He was perfect for her. She didn't need a jumping pony, she needed Harry who would look after her as he had done all week. Nothing could fill the hole left by her mom, but the piebald cob would be someone Ellie could love, and who would love her back, just like—my thoughts flew back to Drummer. Did I still have his love after a week with Catriona? My heart skipped a beat and I hastily turned my attention back to the day's events.

"I can't believe how great this gymkhana has been," I told Sprout. "Everyone's won something—it's amazing!"

"Yeah, amazing, that's the word!" Sprout murmured. "Every week it's the same and everyone thinks things just work out. Extraordinary!"

"Well, they do! I mean, who would have imagined at the beginning of the week that we'd each go home with a blue ribbon, or that Grace, Grace no less, would win the jumping?"

"Who indeed!" snorted Sprout, looking me in the eye. "What do you think our meeting last night was about?!"

CHAPTER 19

ICOULDN'T PEDAL FAST ENOUGH to get to the yard—I couldn't wait to see Drummer's bay face, his cute, inward pointing ears, and liquid brown eyes. Sprout was lovely, but Drum's the one-and-only pony for me!

Grabbing his harness, I ran to the field and spotted him under a tree in the far corner, grazing with Bluey.

"Drum!" I yelled, waving the harness to get his attention. "Drummer, I'm back!"

Every equine head jerked upward to see what all the commotion was about. Except for one. Drummer's.

My heart sank and I set off to get him. Had the worst happened? Had Catriona replaced me in my pony's heart?

"Oh, hello," he said with exaggerated politeness when I got closer. "You managed to find your way back, did you?"

"Oh, Drum, I've missed you so much!" I told him, flinging my arms round his neck and hugging him. He seemed small and chunky and solid after Sprout.

He shook his head and snorted, trying to be angry with me, but after two apples, a carrot, and six sugar lumps, he had almost forgotten he was sulking.

"And I'm so sorry," I told him, leading him to the gate. "Katy was supposed to look after you, I would never have left you with Catriona, you know that. I was devastated when I discovered she was looking after you. How was it? You can tell me." I held my breath, waiting for his answer.

"Fantastic!" snorted Drummer. "I was pampered like never before, let me tell you. Look at my hooves"—he pointed a front toe—"oiled every day. See my ears?" A furry, red, black-tipped ear was shoved in my face. "Clean as a new-born foal's. That girl gave me five-star treatment—I won't have a word said against her!"

"Oh!" I said, my mind churning. I couldn't believe this was happening—Drummer singing Cat's praises. What was I going to do? I chewed my lip.

"Yup, standards have definitely improved," Drummer continued, walking with a spring in his step, tearing my heart to shreds. "The bar has been raised—sky high! I now know how fancy, prize-winning horses feel," he went on, "and as for the treats—they came thick and fast, morning, noon, and night. That Cat knows what a pony likes. Oh yes, I wouldn't have minded if you'd stayed at that place another week. Are you thinking of going again?"

Stopping to face my pony I put my hands squarely on my hips, tipped my head to one side and sucked in my cheeks.

Drummer stared back at me, a picture of equine innocence. "What?" he asked, drawing himself up and sticking his nose in the air, his ears all a twitch, eyes wide, a perfect picture of equine indignation.

I fixed him with my best "you're so busted, mister" look.

He slumped like a pricked balloon. "I went too far, didn't I?" he sighed. "What did it?"

"The treats," I told him. "Morning, noon, and night? You had to push it, didn't you?"

"Oh, it was worth a try. You almost fell for it."

"Dream on!"

"Cat did do a good job, though," Drummer said, stepping into his stable. "Look."

I looked. Drum's straw bed looked so luxurious I would have slept on it. His manger was spotless, his full feed bag tied neatly. It was a model stable. Annabelle would have scribbled ten-out-of-ten on her clipboard if she'd seen it, that much was certain.

"See?" said Drum smugly, digging in to his hay.

"Didn't you miss me at all?" I dared to ask him, slipping off his harness and bolting his door behind us.

"Miss you?" he asked incredulously between chews. "Miss you?"

I sat down in the corner, content just to watch my gorgeous pony munch. I had to win Drum's heart again, I could see that, but it was great to be back. James would soon arrive, Dee would fill Bean and me in with five days' worth of gossip, and, of course (gulp!), I had to thank Catriona for looking after Drummer. I had a present for her in my bag and was determined to try to strike up a conversation—of sorts. Harry had said that people react depending on how you treat them. Perhaps if I was nice to Cat, we could enjoy some sort of truce. I needed to work at it. I hoped the butterflies in my stomach would subside by the time I saw Cat, but I just knew they were going to get worse. I wished Cat would arrive soon so I could get it over with. Pulling out my cell phone, I texted Katy and asked her whether she wanted me to do anything for Bluey, anything to take my mind off what was to come.

A big, furry, black muzzle appeared in front of my nose, and pony breath wafted over my cheeks.

"Hey," said Drum softly. "You can do it, you know."

"Do what?" I asked him, snapping my phone shut.

"What you're worrying about. Just screw up all your courage and get it over with."

"How do you know these things?" I whispered. Drummer was always one step ahead of me, like he was psychic or something.

Drummer let out a sigh. "I've told you before, it's a pony thing," he said. "It's what we do."

"Oh."

"And," continued Drum, his muzzle still hovering near my face, "did I mention that I'm, uh, well, sort of glad you're back?"

"No, you didn't!" I laughed, kissing his nose.

"No, well, I'm a pony of few words," said Drum and went back to his feed bag.

COMING SOON...

The Pony Whisperer

THE PONY REBELLION

CHAPTER 1

"OK, COME CLEAN, WHAT have you all done wrong?" asked James, running his hand through his dark blond hair so that it stood up on end.

"Nothing," said Katy, "but thanks for the vote of confidence—NOT! Besides, we might ask you the same thing!"

"I feel as though I've done something—even though I know I haven't," sighed Bean. "Uh, Pia, what's my feed scoop doing on your hay bales?"

"You left it there," I told her, trying not to look at James. I go a bit funny whenever he does that thing with his hair and I was scared someone else would notice. "You're always leaving stuff on my hay."

"Am I? I wondered where that had gone," Bean mumbled, casually lobbing her scoop back toward her corner of the barn—everyone had a sectioned-off part in the building where they kept their own pony's feed and bedding. The scoop disappeared into the black hole of empty feed sacks, baler twine, and buckets that littered Bean's domain. It was easily the untidiest bit of the barn and so very Bean.

"What did Sophie say to you, Pia?" Katy asked, tying her red hair back behind her head with a band.

"She just said to be in the barn at ten o'clock Saturday

because she had something important to say," I told her, remembering that Sophie had winked when she'd told me, which I had found kinda weird.

"Mmmm, that's what she said to me, too," Katy said, frowning. "What do you think she's up to?"

"She's late, anyway," remarked James, looking at his watch. "If she's not here in two minutes, I'm gone. Anyone wanna come riding with me? I thought I'd take Moth up to Badger's Copse then back via the sloping field."

"So you're in on whatever it is too, are you?" asked Katy.

"Of course!"

"I'll come riding with you," I told James.

"Mmm, me too," said Katy.

"Count me in," added Bean. "I couldn't ride last night so Tiffany will be fresh. Plus it's cold today, so she'll be even livelier."

It was cold, the sort of dry cold that usually follows a heavy frost. The sun was out but it was too early in the morning to compete successfully against the chill. Even in the barn I could see my breath hanging in the air like mini clouds as I spoke—but I love frosty mornings, they're so much better than those dank, dark, dismal, drizzly days which put everyone in a bad mood, especially me. It was early November and the ponies were all clipped and in at night. I thought of Drummer, rugged up and warm in his stable. He was bound to give me a buck or two on our ride before settling down, especially if the other ponies were fresh, too. I'd have to keep my knees in and my heels down if I wanted to keep admiring the scenery, instead of sitting on it!

Suddenly, we heard a car in the drive. Two doors slammed shut.

"At last!" said James as Dee-Dee and her mom, Sophie, appeared at the barn doorway. "Now perhaps we'll find out what the big secret is!"

But Sophie, as usual, was on her cell phone. "Yes, OK," she said, nodding (don't know why, whoever she was talking to couldn't see her). "I'm just about to ask them now. Yes, that's right. No worries. Absolutely. Sure thing. I'll get back to you directly, Linda, and let you know what we'll be doing. Sure. OK…"

Dee-Dee looked at us all and rolled her eyes. I heard James sigh. Well, it was more of a *huff*, really. And then someone I didn't want to see walked through the barn door.

"Hi, Cat!" said Katy. "Are you in on this big mystery as well?"

"What mystery?" Cat asked, her short, dark hair sticking up in that sassy way it does, giving her the sort of air about her that stops you from messing with her. "Sophie just asked me to be here at ten so here I am."

My heart sank. Catriona and I do not get along. Actually, that's an understatement; we don't get along in spectacular style. In the past, Cat has plotted against me, plotted against Drummer, and wasted no opportunity to diss me to anyone passing. She used to go out with James (which was the perfect way to get to me—only

I'd die if anyone knew that), which means that things are sometimes a bit strained between the two of them now, and she's the only negative at Laurel Farm, where I keep Drum. Oh, and she's adamant that I am not a pony whisperer—even though I can totally hear what horses and ponies are saying (under one important condition) and everyone else is on board with it. I think that's our relationship in a nutshell.

Except that when I went away on a riding holiday with Bean in the spring, leaving my beloved Drummer in the capable hands of Katy, it was Cat—through a cruel twist of fate—that ended up looking after him. And, naturally, I then had to thank her when I returned, especially as she'd looked after him really well. When I'd thanked her and given her the gift I'd intended to give to Katy, Cat had shrugged her shoulders, mumbling an OK at me. It had been awkward. Since then we've gone back to avoiding one another.

Sophie finally snapped her phone shut and looked around at us all. "Thanks so much for coming," she began, smiling. She was wearing riding clothes and looked very glamorous—something people in the show ring circuit seem to be able to do without effort. "I have a proposition to make to you all."

"Isn't that something to do with English?" Bean whispered to me, on planet Bean, as per usual.

"That's a preposition," I whispered back. "I think."

"My friend Linda is manager at the local branch of

the Riding for the Disabled Association. You've probably heard of it," Sophie began.

We all nodded.

"Well, Linda is putting on an Equestrian Extravaganza in their indoor school at Christmas to raise funds and she's asked me to organize an event to be included…"

"If Sophie thinks I'm baking cakes or selling programs she's crazier than I thought," James whispered to me under his breath, "and that would be saying something because I already think she's crazier than a box of frogs."

"Shhh," I said. I thought Sophie was bonkers, too, but she was bonkers in a totally horsey way so I forgave her.

"…so I thought it would be wonderful for everyone here to take part in a musical activity ride and perform it on the night of the Extravaganza," Sophie concluded. "It's for a fabulous cause, it will be tremendous fun, and I'm sure you'll all get a lot out of it."

I haven't told you everything about Dee-Dee's mom, have I? She isn't the sort of person you say no to, even if you wanted to. She has a show horse called Lester and Dee shows her pony, dappled gray Dolly Daydream, at all the top shows. Not just for fun—Sophie is totally serious about it, and poor Dee is always having lessons when she'd rather be out riding with us. Only Dolly's worth a pretty penny so she can't—mainly because we're always flying around the countryside out of control.

As Sophie finished speaking, Dee looked puzzled. "Are you including me?" she asked.

"Yes, of course!" Sophie replied briskly, as though Dee was simple.

"Who am I going to ride?"

"Dolly of course. Who do you think?"

"Really?" Dee's jaw dropped. "How come?"

"All the practices will be on soft ground in the school so there should be no problem with her legs," her mother replied. "Honestly, Dee, who else would you ride?"

"It sounds like a great idea," enthused Katy. "But what exactly is an activity ride?"

"It's a musical ride where you'll go over small jumps in different formations. I'll give you all a letter explaining it for you to take home and get your parents to sign. They have to be totally on board with you all doing it and agree to the practices as well as the performance. Obviously you won't need one, Dee," she added.

"It sounds really cool!" cried Bean, suddenly enthusiastic.

"You mean I can jump Dolly?" Dee asked incredulously.

"Yes, Dee. They're only tiny ones—bunny hops—stop going on about it!" said Sophie impatiently.

"It's a miracle!" breathed Dee, falling backward on a hay bale in a mock faint, completely flabbergasted.

Dee wasn't the only one who was surprised—I couldn't believe Sophie was being so casual about Dolly either. It was unheard of.

"Count me in," said James. "Just let me know what you want me to do and I'll be there with Moth. The RDA is a fantastic cause and it sounds like a great thing to do."

"Me, too," said Bean. "There's no way Tiffany and me are being left out!"

"Wild horses wouldn't prevent Bluey and me from being in it, too!" agreed Katy, bouncing up and down on a feed sack in excitement.

"And me," I said. It sounded like fun—I'd always wanted to do something like it, and now here was my chance. I felt a tiny flutter of excitement in the pit of my stomach. I pictured Drum and me sailing over jumps in style, bursting through hoops of paper, soaring through jumps of fire. I imagined a packed audience clapping and cheering for us all in admiration. It would be like being on a TV reality show or something. I mean, how fantastic!

"You can definitely include me and Bambi," said Cat enthusiastically.

The flutter of excitement inside me died, plummeting like it had been shot, and I chewed the inside of my cheek. How was that going to work, me and Cat on a team together? Riding together? Practicing together? Oh for goodness' sake, I thought, we could stay at opposite ends of the ride and make like the other wasn't there. I was sure that would work.

It had to work. I wasn't going to be the only one not included in Sophie's activity ride—it sounded too much like fun!

ABOUT THE AUTHOR

Janet Rising's work with horses has included working at a donkey stud, producing show ponies, and teaching both adults and children, with a special interest in helping nervous riders enjoy their sport, as well as training owners how to handle their horses and ponies from the ground. Always passionate about writing, Janet's first short story was published when she was fourteen, and for the past ten years she has been editor of *PONY*, Britain's top-selling horsy teen magazine.